Long Way Home

Long Way Home

MICHAEL MORPURGO

EGMONT

EGMONT

We bring stories to life

First published in Great Britain in 1975 by Macmillan Education Ltd
This edition published 2012 by Egmont UK Limited
The Yellow Building, 1 Nicholas Road, London W11 4AN

Text copyright © 1975 Michael Morpurgo
Cover illustration copyright © 2006 Oliver Burston

The moral rights of the author and cover illustrator have been asserted

ISBN 978 0 6035 6838 1

A CIP catalogue record for this title is available from the British Library

Printed and bound in Great Britain by the CPI Group

55241/1

MIX
Paper
FSC FSC® C018306

EGMONT LUCKY COIN

Our story began over a century ago, when seventeen-year-old
Egmont Harald Petersen found a coin in the street.

He was on his way to buy a flyswatter, a small hand-operated
printing machine that he then set up in his tiny apartment.

The coin brought him such good luck that today Egmont has
offices in over 30 countries around the world. And that lucky
coin is still kept at the company's head offices in Denmark.

For Clare

CHAPTER 1

THE CAR PURRED COMFORTABLY AND GEORGE was bored with looking out of the window. He glanced down as Mrs Thomas changed gear, and he noticed that she had rather fat legs. She wore thick stockings that wrinkled at the ankles. He didn't like fat legs. Mrs Thomas had been his social worker for as long as he could remember, but he'd never noticed her legs before. She half turned her head, and George looked away quickly, hoping she hadn't seen him staring. He felt his face flush, but it went away quickly.

'They're really very nice people, George,' she said. 'I've known them for years now. I know you'll like Mr and Mrs Dyer. They work on the farm all by themselves, you know. Must be very hard work, I should think. Could do with some help, I expect. You've never lived on a farm before, have you, George?'

'No,' said George.

'There'll be a lot for you to learn. They'll keep you busy, I shouldn't wonder.'

'I told you, I don't want to go.'

'But George, there's hardly anyone left at the Home – no one your age, anyway. They're all on holiday.' She changed gear badly again and the Mini juddered along painfully at twenty miles an hour in top gear.

'I don't care,' George muttered.

'And anyway it's good for you to get away sometimes – good for everyone. We all need a change, don't we?'

'When can I come back?'

'Try not to think of that, George. You'll enjoy it, really you will.'

'When?' George insisted, turning to look at her.

'Well, term starts again early in September – you'll have to go back for that; but they're nice people, George, it's a lovely place and I know they're looking forward to having you.'

Mrs Thomas had known George all his life – ever since he first came to live at the Home when he was three years old, and this was a conversation she had been through with him every time she'd taken him to new foster parents. She knew her credibility must be wearing very thin. Every time they were going to be 'nice people' in a 'good home'. Every time he said he didn't want to go. And every time he was back in the Home within a year, sometimes within a month. He'd run away twice – back to the Home. In all there had been six sets of foster parents, but for one reason or another none of them had worked out: either they hadn't liked him because he was too quiet and sullen, or more often he just hadn't taken to them. It all made anything she said sound hollow and weak, but she had to say something.

'September? But that's over four weeks away.'

Mrs Thomas tried to ignore the despair in his voice and concentrated on the road; there was nothing else she could say about it, nothing that would help.

'Would you like the radio on?' she asked. But George said nothing; he was looking out of the window again. She leaned forward and switched it on anyway – anything was better than this silence.

'Do I have to, Mrs Thomas?' George was pleading now. 'Do I have to go?'

'Let's give it a try, George,' she said. 'It's only for the holidays after all, and you never know, you may have a wonderful time. Just give them time to get to know you – you'll be all right.' She knew George well enough by now to know that he'd lapse into a long silence until they arrived. She was bad at small talk and he had never responded to it, so she reached forward again and turned up the radio, filling the car with the raucous sound of a Radio One jingle and obliterating the silence that had fallen between them.

Tom pushed away his cereal bowl and began to butter his piece of toast. 'What time's he coming?' he said, pushing the butter angrily into the holes in the toast.

'I don't know, dear. Some time mid-morning, I think,' said his mother.

'Every year we do it, Mum. Do we have to do it every year? There must be other people . . .'

'We've been through all this before, Tom,' said his mother, leaving the stove with a plate of sausages.

'You said you wouldn't make a fuss this time – we

agreed.' A door banged upstairs. 'Please, Tom. Dad's coming down – don't go on about it.'

The door was pushed open, and Tom's father came into the kitchen in his dressing-gown and slippers. 'Those calves, they'll have to be moved,' he said, stroking his chin. 'I hardly shut my eyes last night with all that mooing.' He pulled the newspaper out of the back door letter-box, shook it open and sat down.

'And I suppose you'll want me to move them,' said Tom, looking at the picture on the back page of the newspaper and thinking that the Prime Minister looked about the same age as his father. The Prime Minister's face folded up in front of him as his father lowered the paper.

'It's Saturday, isn't it?' Tom knew what was coming. 'I give you five pounds for working weekends on the farm in the summer holidays, five pounds! I run this farm by myself, we've no other help . . .'

'Dad, I didn't mean it like that . . .' But it was no use.

'And it's not as if you even put in a full two days, and every time I ask you to do anything extra, you gripe about it. Your mother and me, we . . .'

'Dad, I was just asking, that's all, just asking if you

wanted me to move those calves.' Tom felt his voice rising in anger and tried to control it. 'Now, do you want me to move them or not?'

'That's not what it sounded like to me,' his father said, retreating a bit.

'Oh, do stop it, you two. Storme's awake, you know – she'll hear you,' said Tom's mother and she scuffled across the kitchen floor towards them with the teapot in one hand and a jug of milk in the other. 'Pour yourselves a cup of tea and do eat your sausages, Tom; they'll be cold.'

'She's heard us before, Mum,' said Tom. 'She's used to it.'

Tom's sister, Storme, thundered down the stairs, the kitchen door banged open and she came hopping in, pulling on a shoe that had come loose.

'It's today, isn't it?' she said, scraping back her chair.

'What is dear?' said her mother.

'That boy, that foster boy,' she said. 'He's coming today, isn't he?'

'Storme, I told you,' her mother said, sitting down for the first time that morning. 'I told you, you're not to call him that. You call him by his name, and his name's George.'

'It's not her fault, Mum,' Tom said, stabbing at the sausage with his fork and looking for the softest place to make an incision. 'Every summer I can remember we've had a foster child living with us, and they've all had different names.'

'Well this one's called George, and don't you forget it,' the newspaper said. The Prime Minister had his legs back again.

'Why do we do it, Mum?' Storme asked, scraping the last drop of milk from the bottom of her cereal bowl.

'Do what, dear?'

'Have all these foster children.'

'I don't really know, dear. I suppose it was your Auntie Helen who started it when she was a probation officer in Exeter – years ago now, before we had you. She suggested we might have a foster child out here for a few weeks in the summer – Anne was the first one, about your age now – and after that the habit just stuck. They wouldn't get a holiday otherwise, you know.'

'You don't know how lucky you are,' said her father.

'Lucky!' said Tom. 'What about last year then? That

girl Jenny, she wouldn't talk to anyone but Mum, you only had to look at her and she'd cry and she never stopped fighting with Storme.'

'You're a fine one to talk,' his mother said.

'Oh, come on, Mum, she was a bloody nuisance – you know she was.'

'Tom!'

'Well, she was,' Tom said. 'And what about the time she left the gate of the water-meadow open, "by mistake" she said, and let all the sheep out?' Tom's mother tried to pour herself another cup of tea. Tom watched as the tea trickled away to tea-leaves.

'She was only young, Tom,' she said quietly, 'and a city girl at that.' She filled the teapot, pulling her head away as the steam rose into her face. 'And if I remember rightly,' she went on, 'it was you that left the tractor lights on all night last Saturday, wasn't it?' Tom knew she was right, but that just made him feel more resentful.

'Anyway,' he said, 'Dad said we wouldn't do it again after her.'

'I said nothing of the kind,' his father said, folding the newspaper. 'I said we should choose more carefully next time, that's all – someone older, more adaptable.'

'And George is twelve, Tom,' said his mother, 'nearly your age. Mrs Thomas says he's a nice boy – shy and quiet, but nice. He just hasn't managed to settle anywhere.' She was scraping off the jam Tom had left on the butter. That was something else Tom and his father were always quarrelling about: dirtying the butter. She hated it when they argued.

'What's "adaptable"?' Storme asked, but no one answered her. She was used to that, so she tried again, pulling at her mother's elbow. 'Mum, Mum, what's "adaptable" mean?' But her mother wasn't listening to her, and Storme wasn't that interested anyway, so she gave up and went back to her sausage.

'I wonder why though?' Tom asked.

'Why what?' his mother said.

'Why he didn't settle anywhere else?'

'Well, I don't know,' Tom's mother said. 'Mrs Thomas didn't say.'

'She wouldn't, would she?' Tom said.

'Now what exactly do you mean by that?' There was an edge to his father's voice.

'Well, if there was something wrong about him, she wouldn't tell you, would she? You wouldn't have him, would you?' Tom looked deliberately at his mother. He was trying to avoid another confrontation with his father. 'Anyway,' he went on, 'she always sends us the worst cases, you know that. You're the only ones that'll take them.'

'That's enough, Tom,' said his mother, but Tom ignored the plea in her voice. He didn't want this George to stay in the house. There had been only one foster child he'd got on with, and he'd been taken away after two weeks because they'd found a permanent home for him somewhere else. The rest of them had just been a nuisance. George might be more his own age than most of them, but somehow that made it worse, not better.

'I can tell you one thing,' Tom said, pushing his sausage plate away. 'I'm not going to look after him all the time, I can tell you that.'

'Please, Tom!' His mother was leaning towards him begging him to stop, but Tom couldn't respond to her – it had gone too far already.

'I've got better things to do,' he said, and as he said it, he knew it sounded a challenge to his father.

'Like working on the farm, I suppose. Moving calves, perhaps?' His father was speaking quietly. Tom recognised the warning sign, but ignored it. It was his holiday they were interfering with and there was only one summer holiday each year.

'I don't want him here. I've got my own friends, haven't I? He'll just be in the way, and what's more you never even asked me about it. It was all arranged between you and Dad and that Mrs Thomas. You're not going to look after him, I am – and no one bothered to ask me, did they?'

'That's not fair, Tom.' His mother sounded hurt, and Tom looked at her. She looked away and began piling up the plates, avoiding Tom with her eyes. 'You know very well I asked you about having another one this summer, and you agreed – well, you said you didn't mind anyway. Anyhow when Mrs Thomas rang up and told me about George, I had to say yes.'

He hadn't meant to upset his mother and he didn't want to go on, but he couldn't bring himself to finish without a final gesture of protest. He scraped back his chair and stood up. And then his father took the wind out of his sails.

'You've said enough.' His father was glaring up at him. 'You're always saying that we treat you like a child. Just listen to yourself. You carry on like a six-year-old.'

'When's he coming?' Storme asked, apparently oblivious of the anger on the other side of the table. It was a fortunately-timed question. Tom and his father were steamed up and ready for battle. Her mother took the opportunity with both hands. 'Mid-morning,' she said hastily. 'She said they'd be here some time around elevenish. It would be nice if all of us could be here to meet him – don't you think, Tom?'

Tom knew she hated his arguments with his father, but it had been better this holiday so far – hardly one serious quarrel until now. He'd managed to control his temper and even his father seemed less inclined to provoke a row. He looked down at his mother and saw in her face that weary, beseeching smile he'd seen so often when she was trying to bring a truce between them.

'I'll be there, Mum,' he said, pushing his chair in.

'You'll be nice to George, dear, won't you?' she went on. 'Give him a chance to settle, eh?' Tom nodded.

'Where do you want those calves, Dad?' he asked, bending down by the door to pull on his boots.

'They'll have to go down on the water-meadows until the winter, I reckon. And Tom, don't forget to check the electric wire down there, will you? We don't want them running around in the woods.' His tone was gentler now. Tom felt it and warmed to it. The trouble was that he was too close to his father – they were too alike in many ways. He stamped his feet firmly into the bottom of his boots. 'What about the milk this morning? Did you do all right?' his father asked.

'Not bad,' said Tom, 'just under two gallons. My wrists are still aching – they'll never get used to it. I took my transistor over like you said and she seemed to like it, but I wish they wouldn't give the news so often – Emma doesn't seem to like it. I think she's bored with it.'

'Sensible cow,' his father laughed.

'Can I come?' Storme was pushing the last crust of toast into her mouth. She always left the crusts till last, always had done. 'I've finished,' she said, wiping her mouth and chewing hard.

'You can open gates if you like,' said Tom. 'I'll see you down there.'

It was as if there had never been a row – better in a way, he thought. He hardly ever thought about his parents unless he'd had a quarrel. He smiled at them and shut the kitchen door behind him. It was blazing hot already and he stood for a moment squinting in the sunlight, then he scuffed his way across the yard, climbed the gate by the Dutch barn and sauntered slowly down the track towards the water-meadows. He kicked at a large piece of silver-black flint that lay in his path, unbuttoned his shirt and wondered about George.

George looked out of the window of the Mini; there was nothing else to do. The grass and the white heads of the hogweed leaned over into the lane ahead of them and bent suddenly in the wind that the car made as it passed. The radio prattled on: 'Well, well, welcome all you lovely people out there on this sunny, sunny day. And for a sunny day, let's all of us listen in to the new sunny sound of "Tin Pan O'Malley" in their amazing, chart-topping new release . . .' Mrs Thomas turned down the volume a little and smiled at him. He liked Mrs Thomas; she was one of the few people he'd known all his life. He was glad she'd stopped trying to talk to him, but she was always good that way.

The familiar dread of meeting new people welled

up inside him. He bit at his knuckle until it brought the tears to his eyes. If only she'd turn round and go back.

'How much further?' he asked.

'Not far now,' she said. 'Two or three miles – won't be long.'

George studied the grooves his teeth had made in his knuckle and the music changed to the hiss of static as they passed under a mesh of electric wires.

George looked out of the window again for the first glimpse of yet another home.

CHAPTER 2

THE CAR RATTLED OVER A CATTLE GRID, AND MRS Thomas slowed down to a crawl, struggling with the gear lever.

'This is it, George,' she said. 'Just down the bottom of the drive,' and the car bobbed and rocked in the craters and ridges of the farm track that led downhill towards a cluster of buildings. George was thrown violently against the door as the Mini keeled over in a rut.

'Sorry about that,' said Mrs Thomas, who was clinging to the wheel rather than driving. 'You all right? It's worse every time I come here.'

George rubbed the side of his head and stiffened

himself for the next crater. It was then that he caught sight of a dark-haired girl, sitting on a gate-post in front of the buildings.

Storme watched the car rocking down the track towards her leaving a trail of dust rising into the air behind it. She hadn't been waiting long. She'd become bored with standing in the sun, holding gates for Tom; and anyway she always liked to see the foster children first – a sort of sneak preview so that she could run in and tell everyone what he was like. She jumped down off the gatepost and tried to make out the features of the boy in the passenger seat, but there was too much dust and the car was still too far away.

'Who's that?' George asked.

'That's the girl I told you about, remember? That's Storme. Looks as if she's been waiting for you.'

The car ground to a halt in the gravel and Storme came towards the car, waving the dust cloud away from her face. She bent down by Mrs Thomas' window.

'Is that him?' she said.

'Hullo, Storme,' said Mrs Thomas, smiling at Storme's bluntness. 'This is George. George, this is Storme.'

Storme peered across Mrs Thomas and scrutinised

George, who stared back. Like a parcel, he thought, it's just like a postman delivering a parcel.

'Your mum and dad?' Mrs Thomas felt for George. 'Are they in the house?'

'Think so,' said Storme, who was beaming at George by now. 'You drive up. I'll go and tell everyone he's here.'

George watched her run off shouting at the top of her voice. 'Always the same,' he muttered. 'They always stare at you.'

'Come on, George,' said Mrs Thomas. 'She's only young. She's interested, that's all; and after all, you are a new face.'

The car bumped across the farmyard scattering ducks and chickens in all directions and disturbing a sparrow that was having a dust-bath in one of the ruts. The car pulled up with a jerk. She turned off the engine.

'Do try to enjoy yourself, George,' she said before she opened the door, but George wasn't listening. He was absorbed by a white duck that was waddling away from the car, sideways like a crab, keeping one eye on him and the other on the chorus of indignant hens in front of her. The main flock of ducks huddled together in noisy confusion against a brick wall: this one quacked out her own special defiance. George winked at her. She seemed offended and waddled off, bottom-heavy and cumbersome, towards the pond.

And then he was standing beside the hot car and Mrs Thomas was smiling thinly and making the introductions. Storme was clutching her mother's hand, pulling her forward, and her father trailed along behind. They were all smiling at him. No one said anything. There were some sheep bleating in the distance and a chicken jerked its way between George and the car, pecking at the dust and warbling softly to herself. George felt hot and wondered what to do with his hands.

'I saw him first, Mum. I told you I would,' said Storme, still beaming at him.

'Hullo, George,' said the smiling lady in the apron. 'You're a bit early. Caught us on the hop – but no matter, it's lovely you're here.'

'Better early than late, lad,' the man said, taking George's suitcase from Mrs Thomas. George's white duck had come back and was standing by the car, watching. George was relieved to have something else to look at. 'Tom's not here at the moment,' Storme's father went on. 'Still out with the calves, I shouldn't wonder.' George stared back at his duck and wondered if ducks ever blinked.

'Shall we go and get him?' said Storme, trying to make George look at her. She wondered what he saw in the duck.

'That's a good idea,' Mrs Dyer said. 'He's down in the water-meadows somewhere, and we'll give Mrs Thomas a cup of coffee – all right?' George nodded and tried a smile that didn't happen.

Storme didn't have to be asked twice. 'Come on,' she said, and ran past him. George looked at Mrs Thomas who smiled and then walked away with Mr and Mrs Dyer. They'd be talking about him. 'Come on,' Storme was shouting at him from the gate. They climbed over and walked down the dusty track towards the water-meadows.

'Mind the cows,' said Storme, pointing at the ground by George's feet. The warning was only just in time and George managed to lengthen his stride and avoid the huge cowpat that was spread out at his feet. He looked at her and they both laughed together. Then a fly was after him, buzzing round his ears. He swiped at it, but that just seemed to encourage it.

Storme was prattling on. 'Tom's been chasing calves around all morning.' She was chewing a long piece of yellow grass. 'Last time I saw him, he was all hot and cross. He came back in for a drink just before you came – grumbling about the flies. And do you know? He said his favourite meat was veal. I don't think that's very funny, do you?'

George looked down at her and listened; she never gave him a glance. She could have been talking to herself, until she said suddenly, 'The girl we had last year, she didn't like it here very much.'

'What girl?' George asked.

'Jenny. She was the one we had last time. Mrs Thomas brought her as well. She always brings them. Do you like her?'

'Who?'

'Mrs Thomas,' Storme said, scuffing her feet in the ruts and creating a dust storm round her ankles.

'She's all right,' George said. 'You have someone every summer, do you?'

'Oh, yes,' she went on. 'I don't mind much, but Tom doesn't like it.' George shook his head against the fly and swiped at it again.

'I hate flies,' he said.

'Lots of them here,' said Storme. 'They like the animals, see. You'll get used to them.' She pointed ahead of her and George followed her arm. 'There he is,' she said, and she ran down the track, leaping like a goat from rut to rut. George could see only the top half of Tom; the rest was hidden by the calves that were milling around him.

'Tom! Tom!' she shouted, leaning over the gate and cupping her hands to her mouth. 'It's George! He's here!' Tom waved back from the bottom of the field.

George looked at Storme standing on the bottom rung of the five-barred gate. This was something he had not met before: someone who was completely natural and open. She said just what came into her head; there were no pretensions, no inhibitions. He transferred his attention to the boy in dark jeans who was walking slowly towards them across the field followed closely by a small black and white calf.

'Still looks cross,' said Storme. 'And that's Jemima behind him. Only three months old she is, and she sucks anything she can get hold of.' And she laughed as Tom slapped out behind him at the calf that was doing its best to suck the shirt out of his trousers.

Tom had seen them coming before Storme shouted

to him. He'd been brooding about George all morning. His mind hadn't been on the job. That was why he'd taken so long to bring the calves down into the water-meadows. Somehow Jemima had separated herself from the herd and skipped off before he could stop her. He'd herded the rest of them into the field and had to go back for Jemima. He'd found her munching away happily near the cattle grid at the top of the drive. All the way back down to the water-meadows he'd cursed Jemima and the heat and the flies, and particularly George.

And now here he was tramping reluctantly towards George and Storme, followed by the adoring Jemima who didn't seem to understand that she wasn't wanted. Tom hated meeting people anyway and by the time he got to the gate he still hadn't thought of anything to say. But Storme solved that problem.

'You caught her then?' she grinned at him.

'Yes,' he said. The two boys looked briefly at each other, and then looked away. Neither could bring themselves to say anything.

Then Jemima was at his shirt again, and he turned and pushed her away. He was grateful for the intrusion – it gave him time to think of something to say.

'Don't do that,' said Storme. 'She loves you – you'll hurt her feelings.'

'She hasn't got any,' said Tom. 'If she had, she wouldn't have had me chasing up and down in the heat all morning, would she?' He talked deliberately at Storme, but it was Jemima that finally forced the two boys to acknowledge each other. Repeatedly rejected, Jemima left Tom's shirt and swayed towards George and before he could move, he felt a sharp tug at his trouser leg and looked down. He was being sucked at noisily. He pulled his leg away from the gate, but Jemima pushed her head further through the bars so that George had to step back quickly to avoid her. Storme leaned across offering her hand to Jemima who took it and sucked on it hungrily.

'Like sandpaper, her tongue. Almost sucks your hand off,' said Storme, pulling her hand away and wiping the saliva off on the grass.

'I didn't know they were so friendly,' said George, now safely out of reach of the grey tongue that was still curling out like a tentacle in search of something or someone to suck.

'They're not,' said Tom. 'This one's odd – doesn't like cows at all, just people.' They looked at each other as they spoke and then back at Jemima. Jemima pulled her tongue in and looked up at them with her great gentle eyes. 'Do I look like your mother?' Tom asked Jemima. 'Is that it?' They were all laughing now. Jemima blinked dreamily up at him, stretched her neck upwards and out came the tongue again, but Tom sidestepped her and climbed the gate. They left her forlorn and disappointed, her white head thrust through the gate.

By the time they reached the house, Mrs Thomas had gone. George half-expected it anyway – it was a favourite trick of hers that he knew well by now. She would leave without really saying goodbye, but this time it didn't seem to matter to him that much.

After lunch Storme took him up the dark, narrow staircase to his room at the top of the house, and during the afternoon he helped to unload hay-bales from the trailer and stack them in the Dutch barn with Tom, Storme and Mr Dyer. Storme didn't do much – she just talked. The sun shimmered hot behind a layer of cloud, and as the afternoon went on the air became heavy and the work more exhausting. Storme gave up her chatter and went inside; the hay was tickling her and she couldn't stop coughing and spluttering in the dust thrown up by the bales as they hit the ground.

George worked on, the sweat trickling down into the corners of his eyes. Every time he picked up a bale he winced as the string bit into his fingers. But he was happy listening to Tom and his father chatting. They didn't talk to him much. What he dreaded was when people forced themselves to talk to him – he could always tell. Once or twice he caught Tom looking at him strangely, but then he was doing the same to Tom – sizing him up.

The clouds built up above them as they worked and in the distance there was the rumble of thunder. Shortly after, the rain started, falling in huge drops, slowly at first. Mr Dyer drove the tractor and trailer under cover of the half-filled Dutch barn and they ran back to the house, closing their eyes against the rain that pounded down on them, plastering their hair down flat on to their heads. They burst in laughing through the kitchen door, the water pouring from their noses, their shirts clinging to their backs.

'Not before time,' said Tom's father, shaking his arms. 'We could do with it. First rain for over a month. Things never happen by halves, do they?'

'We got most of it done, anyway,' said Tom, and he

grabbed some drying-up cloths from the rail by the stove. Mrs Dyer rescued them and handed out warm towels instead.

'We should finish stacking next week,' Tom's father said, emerging from the folds of the towel that covered his head. 'Got it done twice as fast with George here. I don't suppose you've got much skin left on your fingers, eh? They'll harden up, don't you worry.' George looked down at his raw hands. He'd forgotten they were hurting. He pulled his shirt off like the others and dropped it over the back of a chair. Then he set to work rubbing his hair dry. The kitchen smelt a bit like a launderette. George screwed up his eyes and rubbed the warmth back into his head.

'And I suppose you'll want paying as well,' Tom's father mumbled from underneath his towel.

George stopped rubbing and lowered his towel. 'Paying?' he said. He looked from Tom to his father, but they were both hidden by their towels. He was confused. It had been a wonderful afternoon; he had felt at ease with everyone. There had been no special treatment. He had begun to feel that he belonged there working with them. And now, suddenly, Mr Dyer was offering to pay him money – just to him, not to Storme or Tom, just to him. He was to be paid for the work like all the other foster children who came there every summer. 'I don't want to be paid,' he said quietly, and he turned away from them and walked out of the kitchen and up the stairs to the privacy of his room.

He sat down on his bed under the window and threw his towel angrily into the corner. It *was* the same after all, just like all the other families, maybe even worse; no one had ever treated him like a hired worker before, and at least you knew where you were with them. He got up and retrieved the towel. He was not going to stay on those terms, not for Mrs Thomas, not for anyone. He took out his dry clothes and pushed his wet trousers and shirt down to the bottom of his case. He would leave during the night; it was easier that way – no arguments, no explanations. He'd done it before. They could find another foster boy to work for them. This time tomorrow, he'd be back in the Home, and maybe Mrs Thomas would listen to him from now on.

There was a knock on his door. 'You in there, George?' It was Storme. George pushed his suitcase under the bed. The latch clicked up. 'You still look wet,' she said. 'Mum said to come down – tea's ready.' George nodded and stood up. Storme ventured further into the room. 'What's the matter?' she asked. 'Don't you like it here? You liked it out in the barn this afternoon – I was watching you. I bet it was Tom. Did he say something? Don't take any notice of him – he's like that. You mustn't take any notice – I don't.'

'I'm all right,' said George.

'Dad said he thought you were cross about something,' she went on.

'Well, I'm not!' George spoke abruptly and Storme was surprised at the harshness in his voice. She led the way downstairs but said nothing more.

All through tea George felt Storme's eyes on him while the others talked among themselves. Occasionally he looked up at her to try to find out what she was thinking, but each time she looked away quickly. It was almost as if she knew what he was planning to do that night. Mr Dyer didn't mention the money again and Tom spoke only once to him to ask him for the tomato ketchup for his fish fingers.

'Been pouring now for some time,' said Mr Dyer, turning round to look out of the window. 'If it goes on like this, we'll have a river down the bottom of the water-meadow instead of a trickle.'

'We'll have the fish back,' said Mrs Dyer. 'You ever been fishing, George?' George shook his head and chased a pea across his plate until he trapped it up against his last fish finger. 'We get brown trout and rainbow trout, all sorts down there,' she said.

The thunder crashed right above them, rattling the windows and bringing the conversation to a halt. The lights flickered nervously. They stopped eating and listened to the rain hammering down on the corrugated roof of the shed outside. It sounded like hailstones.

'The calves won't like this much,' said Tom, going back to his food and dipping some bread in his tomato sauce. 'And that mad Jemima – she'll do her nut.'

'Bound to be lightning. You can feel it in the air,' said Mr Dyer, standing up. 'I'm off to shut up the chickens.'

He was right. There was lightning later that night. Lying on his bed, George watched the sky outside flash white. He knelt up and pressed his face against the teeming window pane above the bed and waited for the next flash. When it came, the countryside turned from black to a lead grey and then back to a deeper black. He watched for some time, wiping the window with his sleeve whenever it became steamed up. Then he climbed into his bed, still fully dressed, and waited. Mrs Dyer called goodnight up the stairs, and Storme came up in her green dressing-gown and matching slippers and said she'd see him in the morning. She waved at him from the door and was gone. He was alone.

He planned to wait until the storm had passed its peak and everyone was asleep. He looked at his hands and examined the red weals and blisters of the day's work. It could have been so good here, he thought. He leaned out of bed and arranged his shoes so that he could find them easily later on. He pulled his case out from underneath the bed and stood it up so that he could find the handle in the dark. He switched off the light and lay back. I should have taken that money, he thought; at least it would have paid my fare back to the Home. Now I've got to hitch all the way.

CHAPTER 3

SOMEONE WAS SHAKING HIM. WEIRD SHADOWS were dancing on the ceiling. Tom was bending over him. 'George, George. Wake up! We've got flooding, George. Wake up!'

George sat up. He'd dropped off to sleep. 'Flooding? What do you mean?' he said.

'The river's burst its banks, and the water-meadow's under water already. I've just been down there. Those calves will drown if we leave them there. We must get them out and I can't do it by myself.'

George tried to collect his thoughts. 'Where's your dad?' he asked finally, staring blankly at the candle flickering in Tom's hand.

'They went out. They've gone to see Grandad. They said they'd be back in an hour, and that was three hours ago. I don't know where they've got to. Come on, George. Hurry up. We haven't got much time.'

George pushed back the covers and swung his feet on to the floor. 'The lights, what's happened to the lights?' he asked, wondering for the first time about the candle.

'Power cut,' said Tom, who was staring at George. 'Must have been the lightning. It always happens when there's a storm. You've got your clothes on,' he said.

George looked down at himself. He'd forgotten about that. 'I know,' he said, standing up. They looked at each other over the light of the candle.

'Come on,' said Tom. 'Those calves.'

They ran downstairs to the kitchen door and Tom gave George his father's coat and boots, but it was only when Tom opened the door and pushed him out into the cold wet of the night that George began to understand what was really happening. He gasped as the wind and the rain lashed his face, and then Tom was ahead of him with a torch and shouting.

'There should be twelve of them,' he yelled against

the wind. 'We'll have to move them back up into to the field behind us. All right?'

George heard only the odd word, but the sense was clear enough. He splashed across the farmyard after Tom who waved the weak torchlight behind him so that George could see where he was going. It didn't help much. He slipped and slid in the ruts and fell twice, face down in the running mud. Each time, Tom stopped and splashed back towards him to help him up.

'The boots!' George shouted. 'It's the boots – they're too big.'

Tom laughed. 'You can take them off if you'd feel better,' he shouted back.

They slithered together down the track after that, the frail pink light of the torch dancing in front of them and telling them nothing of the hazards ahead. All they could see was the rain falling across the beam of light. They held on to each other, so that whenever one felt his legs beginning to slide beneath him, he could clutch the other for support.

Then they could hear the mooing ahead of them in the dark. Tom aimed his torch at the sound, and they stumbled on towards the gate until they saw the white noses of some of the calves on the high ground near the gate. Tom counted aloud. 'There's only ten here,' he shouted, shining the torch over the backs of the calves who were pushing against the gate, mooing in terror. 'Should be twelve!' The torch beam flashed briefly across a pair of frightened white eyes.

'They'll be all right here,' Tom yelled. 'We'll have to find the other two; one of them's Jemima. She's not here. You go that way, but be careful – look!' Tom shone the torch down towards the ground on the other side of the gate. There was no grass; it was all water. He climbed over the gate and pushed his way through the calves. George followed, eyeing them warily. Some of them looked more like little bulls than calves to him. Tom patted him on the shoulder, pointed into the darkness and then he was gone and George was on his own.

Almost immediately George felt himself walking down a slope and into shallow water. He splashed on, straining his eyes ahead of him into the dark. Occasionally he looked back to get his bearings by Tom's torchlight, now a small speck of light in the distance. He pulled the collar of his coat up to stop the steady stream of water that was running down his neck. He could see better now and began to call out into the night. 'Jemima! Jemima! Where are you? Jemima!' He was glad the wind was so strong that no one could hear him – he sounded ridiculous. He was playing hide-and-seek with a calf! Then it occurred to him that there was no point in shouting anyway, because if no one could hear him, then neither could Jemima. He waded further into the field and felt the water coming in over his boots. Every step now the water tugged at his legs and he found it more and more difficult to pick his leg up for the next step: he had to grip with his toes to stop his boots being sucked off. The wind was whipping round his face, stinging his eyes. Then he heard the mooing.

'Coming,' he shouted, turning towards the sound, and he strode out through the water. It was close but he still couldn't see anything.

The water was up around his waist now. Using his arms as paddles he waded on until his foot struck something under the water. He stumbled and tried to regain his balance, but there was no longer any ground under his feet. Until this moment George had not been frightened. At first he had been too sleepy and bewildered, and then too preoccupied with keeping upright to worry about himself. He kicked out again, but again his legs met nothing but water underneath him. He felt himself sinking and struck out with his arms to keep his head above water. Panic gripped him. He cried out. 'Help! I can't swim! I can't swim! Help!' But the water came into his mouth and choked him. He felt his head going under and kicked out wildly. His feet touched solid ground. He pushed himself upright and for some moments he stood there fighting against the current to keep his feet on the ground. He gulped the fresh air like a fish out of water. The moment of blind terror was over. He felt his breath coming more easily and he leaned against the current, fighting to keep his balance. From the darkness behind him came the same plaintive mooing. He turned carefully. The mooing seemed closer now and he peered forward, wiping the rain from his face, and pushing the hair back out of his eyes.

At first the calf was a dull grey shape above the black water-line, but as George waded nearer he could pick out a white head and then the black and white of her back. There was no doubt about it – it was Jemima. She saw him and set up a high-pitched bellow. George didn't know whether it was in gratitude or abuse, so he approached her gingerly. The last time they had met there had been a fence between them.

He felt the ground underneath him rise steeply as he clambered up towards her. He felt his knees break free above the water. He looked round for Tom's torchlight but he could see nothing but the oily black of the water and the dark grey of the sky. He kept his distance and cupped his hands round his mouth. 'Tom! I've found one! Tom! To-o-om! Over here!' His voice cracked. 'To-o-om! It's Jemima. I've found her!' But the wind threw his voice back at him. He listened for a reply from the darkness, but none came. Jemima was sucking at his coat behind him. He turned and patted her neck. She was clearly not a wild beast after all.

George let Jemima suck on, and began to try to find out where the gate to the field was. He searched the skyline looking for some shape he could recognise. He remembered there were trees on the other side of the river – a line of tall thin trees – but there seemed to be tree shapes wherever he looked. Then high in the grey sky he found the trees broken by a long, dark silhouette slightly curved at one end. The Dutch barn! That was at the top of the track that led down to the water-meadow – the gate must be directly below that shape somewhere.

'Come on, then,' he said tentatively, wading backwards away from Jemima. But Jemima didn't move. He backed away again beckoning her to come, and the water was coming into his boots again; he was backing downhill. Jemima had chosen a mound in the field as her sanctuary. George knew that, but he had no idea how to entice her back into the deeper water between them and the gate. He called her again, more firmly this time. She looked at him as if to say, 'You gotta be joking.'

George walked back towards her up the mound, sidled round her and began to push from behind. It was like trying to prise a limpet off a rock. Each time he pushed, he felt Jemima give a little and then she stood firm and immovable, looking back over her shoulder quizzically. He stepped back and then threw his full weight on to her. His feet slipped from under him. In desperation he clutched at Jemima, found her tail and clung on. As he pulled himself up, twisting the tail, he felt Jemima move forward down the slope.

He'd found the right button, the one that made her go. He stumbled after her, clinging on to the tail – nothing was going to make him let go now. Whenever Jemima stopped, George twisted the tail hard and leaned on her, urging her forward.

The deep water did not last long. They were moving up towards the gate when George saw the headlights of a car flash across the sky out over the water-meadows. A car was turning down the track towards the farm. The lights bobbed up and down towards him and then disappeared behind the Dutch barn. His bearings were right. Jemima was moving on without protest now, but even so George still kept a firm hold on her tail. He heard the other calves mooing ahead of him, and then he saw them in a bunch, and Tom was shouting and waving from the gate. Jemima pulled away from him as they reached the mud by the gate and she lost herself among the others.

'You got her!' Tom shouted. 'Where d'you find her?'

George shouted back, pointing back towards the river. 'Down by the river, I think. Stuck on a hill.' George pushed his way through the calves to the gate. 'What about you? Did you find the other one?'

'I got her – she was up by the woods. You been for a swim? Wasn't it wet enough for you?' Tom was laughing.

'I didn't mean to,' George said. 'I tripped.' Tom's laughter was infectious.

'You should see yourself,' Tom said, helping him over the gate. 'That coat – you look like a drowned scarecrow.' And the two of them leaned against the gate and laughed until it hurt, while the calves looked at them wide-eyed and bemused.

'Mum and Dad are back,' said Tom. 'I saw the car. We'll get the calves up the track. I'll whip them up from behind. You make sure they go in the gate. All right?'

George's coat weighed him down as it clung to him cold and heavy. He waited for the calves up by the gate and wondered how he was going to make them all go through. A torch beam cut through the darkness towards him.

'That you, Tom?' It was Mr Dyer's voice.

'It's me,' said George. 'Tom's on his way up with the calves.'

'I'll manage, lad,' said Mr Dyer. 'You go on in and get yourself dry. You'll catch your death out here.' He ran past George waving his torch and calling the calves. George stood and watched them swing past him, nodding their heads with the effort of walking uphill. Last of all came Jemima and she never gave him a glance – she seemed hypnotised by the swinging tail of the calf in front of her.

Inside the house Mrs Dyer pulled the coat off him, emptied his boots down the sink and sent him upstairs to have a bath.

George shivered with pleasure as he felt the warmth rise in waves from his knees to his head. He lay back and savoured it. And then Tom was banging on the bathroom door. 'Hurry up, George. Mum's got a warm drink for us downstairs.'

George sat up. 'Coming,' he said, and he looked around for something to wear, something besides his wet clothes. There was a pile of pyjamas hanging over the towel rail, but they weren't his. 'Tom,' he shouted, hearing the steps going away, 'I haven't got my pyjamas.' The steps came back.

'Mum says she put a pair of mine out for you,' Tom said. 'Don't be too long, and don't let the plug out. I want a soak in there after you.'

Later the four of them sat round the table in the

kitchen, sipping hot chocolate and swopping stories. 'We'd have been back sooner. It was that ruddy car again, wouldn't start,' said Tom's father. 'I never thought the river would come up that fast anyway – never known it before.'

Tom blew on his chocolate and picked off the skin. 'It's a good thing for that Jemima that George was here; she doesn't know how lucky she was.'

George felt everyone looking at him again; but he didn't mind now. He smiled back at Mrs Dyer and warmed his hands round the mug.

'You ever handled cows before?' said Mr Dyer.

'No,' said George.

'John Wayne couldn't have done it better,' Tom said. 'If he'd had a lasso, he'd have roped her in, wouldn't you George?' They laughed and George laughed with them. He scraped the sugar from the bottom of his mug.

'I couldn't find your pyjamas, George,' said Mrs Dyer. 'Couldn't find your suitcase for that matter.' She took his mug. 'You don't mind a pair of Tom's just for now, do you?' George felt Tom looking at him and didn't dare look up.

'Go on, off to bed the two of you,' said Tom's father.

'Don't forget you're on milking again tomorrow, Tom. Sunday, remember?'

'How could I forget?' said Tom.

'George,' said Mrs Dyer as they reached the door, 'thanks for what you did tonight, dear. Tom says he couldn't have done it without you.'

George nodded, smiled at them both and followed Tom upstairs.

Tom stopped at the foot of the stairs the led up to George's room. 'About this afternoon, George,' he said. 'You know, about what Dad said about paying you for helping in the barn. It's only fair, you know; he pays me for doing farmwork at the weekends. It's holiday money; he couldn't very well pay me and not pay you, could he?'

It took George a few seconds to understand what Tom was talking about. He hadn't thought about it once since he'd been woken up. 'You get paid?' he said. 'And Storme?'

'When she does any work – doesn't happen very often,' Tom said, laughing. 'You'll stay now? Unpack your case and go to bed in pyjamas?'

George smiled.

'See you for milking then?' said Tom.

'What time?'

'Early,' Tom said, grinning. 'Goodnight.'

'Goodnight,' said George. He climbed the stairs to his room. He pulled his suitcase out from under the bed and began to unpack.

CHAPTER 4

GEORGE WAS UP IN THE EARLY MISTS THE NEXT morning. There were only two cows and Tom did most of the work anyway, herding them into the shed and chaining them round their necks. George was appointed udder-washer; he had a pail of disinfectant and a rag. Tom gave him a stool and told him to get on with it. He was too sleepy to be frightened even when the first cow moved sideways threatening to barge him off his stool. She gazed down at him, chomping rhythmically and blinking her great black eyes – surprised at his unskilled hand. George had never realised how huge and heavy a cow's udder was – it hung low, almost touching the ground. Tom switched on his transistor radio and disappeared behind the other cow. The shed filled with the crackle of distant pop music and the regular splash of the milk against the side of the pail.

Afterwards Tom gave him a broom and told him to sweep the shed while he turned the cows out to grass. It was heavy work – cows seem to leave a lot behind them in a very short time – and then there was the smell, which made George retch. Tom came back and they hosed the place down together. There were the chickens to feed and water, and the eggs to collect. Then the pigs had to be fed and finally the calves they'd moved the night before. They were all grazing quietly and George spotted Jemima among them on the far side of the field.

'River's down again already,' said Tom as they turned away from the calves to the water-meadows. The river was still twice as wide as it should have been but most of the field was grass again. 'Soaked it up like blotting paper,' Tom said. 'Come on, should be breakfast by now – we've earned it.'

Mrs Dyer was up and breakfast was on the table. They wolfed down their bacon, eggs and toast with hardly a word between them, and by his second cup of tea George was beginning to remember everything that had happened the night before.

'Dad still in bed?' said Tom, sitting back in his chair.

'Fast asleep – his first lie-in for months.'

'And Storme?'

'She'll be down any minute – says she was kept awake last night by the storm,' said Mrs Dyer. 'She wouldn't believe me when I told her about the flood – says she would have heard something.'

'Hiding under her pillow I shouldn't wonder,' Tom said. 'She's petrified of lightning – told me so herself.'

'You leave her be now, Tom – she's cross enough as it is.' She turned to George. 'Have you had enough now, George? You haven't eaten much, you know.' George was about to say that he'd already eaten twice as much as he usually did, when Tom answered for him.

'Udders before breakfast – puts you right off, doesn't it, George? I don't know how Dad does it every morning.' They were still laughing when Storme came down in her dressing-gown, bleary-eyed and yawning.

'Good evening,' said Tom, standing up and bowing low to Storme, who glared at him. 'And how is my lady this morning? Your humble serfs, George here and myself, have milked your cows, fed your chickens and the cook has prepared your breakfast. Would you like it here or in bed, my lady? Tea or coffee? Just say the word.'

'Get knotted,' Storme said, pushing past him to her chair.

'Anything you say, my lady, anything you say.'

George watched them taunting each other and thought of breakfast at the Home. It was always fried bread with something in the cold dining-room downstairs. It was a huge room with a high ceiling and there was a hatch from the kitchen just above the sideboard. After your cereal you waited for the hatch to bang up and that was the signal to fetch your fried bread with something. No one said much – there was just the clinking of knives and spoons and the little ones squabbling down the other end of the table. The smell of floor polish and boiled potatoes was everywhere, and there was a picture of the Queen on the wall which was always crooked.

Storme was talking to him. 'George?'

'Yes?'

'We could go up on to the moor,' she said. 'Have

you been up there? I'm not allowed by myself and no one else ever takes me.'

'Rubbish,' said Tom. 'You were up there with Dad only last week – and anyway I'm on farmwork today, I can't come.'

'Nobody asked you, did they?' said Storme. Tom looked at her sharply and Mrs Dyer intervened in the interests of peace.

'I don't think Dad would mind,' she said, 'not after what you did last night. That was overtime, I should think. You'd like to go up on the moor, wouldn't you George?'

' 'Course he would, Mum,' said Storme quickly.

'Go on Tom, go and ask Dad,' said Mrs Dyer. 'He won't mind, I'm sure he won't.'

His father was propped up in bed, reading. Tom hardly ever saw him in bed. Usually he was up and about hours before anyone else. It didn't seem a natural place for his father to be.

'Everything done?' he said, still reading his book.

'All done.'

'Did you check the calves?' He looked up now.

'We did everything, Dad. I had George with me.'

'What d'you want, then?' he said.

'It's Storme and George – they want to go up on the moor.'

'Well?'

Tom hated asking his father for anything – he always made him feel as if he was begging. 'Someone's got to look after them,' he said. It sounded limp.

'You want time off, don't you, eh?'

'Just the afternoon, Dad, that's all. I'll make it up during the week sometime.'

His father was smiling at him. 'You made it up already – last night. I'll do the milking this afternoon. But before you go off, see if you can finish shifting those bales. All right?' Tom turned to go. 'And Tom, watch the weather. You know the mists can come down quickly this time of year. Get back well before supper.'

'Don't worry, Dad. We'll be all right.'

So they spent the morning stacking the hay in the Dutch barn. The air was fresh and clean from the rain, but the sun was shining hot again in a clear sky. They worked hard all morning building the hay bales right up under the warm corrugated roof, and every half-hour they were refreshed by Storme's over-diluted orange juice. Tom kept sending her off on useless errands just to keep her out of the way; she wasn't strong enough to carry the bales and all she wanted to do was to talk to George. He could feel more at ease with George when she wasn't there showing off about the farm and asking George personal questions.

George was stacking higher up on the bales, so that at times he could reach up and touch the roof. Most of the time Tom was out of sight below him so that talking was like a telephone conversation. George found it easier to talk that way, less direct somehow.

'You been up there before, on the moor?' Tom asked.

'Once or twice – orienteering from school. It rained all the time.'

'Always does, when it's not snowing,' said Tom, sitting down on a broken bale.

'And I've been up there once in the snow – Adventure Training camp, year or so ago. Never again.'

'What? Walking, trekking and all that?'

'Never again. I ran away anyway,' George admitted without thinking about it.

'You what?'

'Ran away. I didn't know anyone there. Didn't want to go in the first place.'

'That's what you packed your case for yesterday, isn't it?' Tom waited for a reply. The long pause worried him – he wondered if the question had been too sudden, too direct.

'You won't tell anyone, will you?' George leaned over a rampart of bales to look down at Tom.

' 'Course not,' Tom said. 'There's lots of times I've wanted to run away from here, I can tell you. But why did you want to?'

'I didn't want to come. Mrs Thomas forced me to – and then there was that money business with your dad.'

'I thought it was that,' Tom said, looking up at him. 'Matter of fact, I didn't want you to come either – that makes two of us.'

George hid behind his bales again and went on. 'I'm always being sent off to stay with new people and they always treat me like I'm odd or something, you know, different or special. I thought it was going to be the same here.'

'We've had too many foster children – Mum's idea – and I didn't want another one, that's all,' Tom said.

'Storme told me – 'bout the first thing she told me.' He heard Tom laughing below him. 'I like it here,' George went on. 'No one pretends here.'

Storme was shouting up at them from the ground. 'Fat lot of work you're doing up there. I'll leave the orange juice here. Don't work too hard, will you?'

'Sweet, isn't she?' said Tom, grinning up at George. He shouted after Storme. 'Hope there's some orange in it this time.' Storme didn't look back.

Storme felt hurt inside as she walked away. If George hadn't been there, she'd have screamed at Tom. The night before she had gone to bed thinking about George and about how he liked her, much more than he did the rest of the family. She knew Tom didn't want George in the house, and George seemed to be more friendly with her than with anyone else. But overnight everything had changed; George and Tom had become inseparable now. She'd missed the rescue last night, and by the time she was up the two of them had already been working together for hours. She tried to talk to George, but Tom always answered and made her feel young and silly. She tried to catch his eyes, but he never seemed to be looking at her. She resented Tom's new-found enthusiasm for George and the way he clearly enjoyed George's company. She knew Tom was only trying to keep her away from George so that he could keep him to himself. But this afternoon there was a chance; they were going on to the moor and she knew the moor better than Tom, who only ever went up there to fish or to swim, and that wasn't very often. It would be better up there; she'd have a chance to talk to George alone.

The sun blazed that afternoon and the flies came out in their millions to follow George on to the moor. The ground was springy under his feet; it felt like layer upon layer of grass and moss. Storme had been prattling on beside him since they left the farm. He'd stopped listening a long time ago – not because he was bored with her, but because she seemed to be talking more to herself than to anyone else. She was giving a panoramic guide of the moor – the bogs, the ponies, the sheep, the buzzards, the rivers, the tors, the stone circles. Tom walked ahead of them with the haversack. George watched it bouncing up and down on his back.

'We're going to the river,' said Tom over his shoulder. 'Should be full again after last night.'

'How far is it?' George asked, his feet hurting already.

'About an hour or so,' Tom said.

'We always go there,' Storme moaned. 'There's nothing to do there except swim. Why can't we take George up to the stone circle? It's not much further.'

'We haven't got time, and anyway that place is always full of sheep's muck. I think they come from all over Dartmoor to do it there.' Tom laughed and hitched up the haversack.

George felt sorry for Storme and asked her about the stone circles. He should never have done it. She was still going on about them by the time they reached the river.

Tom ran down the slope to the river, pulled off his clothes and leapt into the water screaming like a marauding Viking. The other two stood and watched.

'Come on in,' he shouted. Storme looked at George, who was smiling weakly.

'You go,' he said. 'I'll wait here.'

'I'm not going in there – it's freezing,' said Storme.

'What's the matter?' Tom was shouting and waving. He plunged like a porpoise and reappeared on the far bank. 'Come on. It's lovely.'

George turned away from Storme and walked back up the hill. She came after him.

'What's the matter?' she said.

'Nothing,' he snapped. 'Nothing.'

George was dreading the questions. Up till now he'd managed to avoid swimming. He was always losing his bathing costume at school, or having ear-ache – something, anything to avoid having to go in. Storme was panting up through the bracken behind him, and he could see Tom thrashing up the hill behind her.

'George?' Storme said, catching him up.

'I can't swim,' he said.

'What about last night?' Tom said, pushing his wet hair away from his face. 'I had flood water up to my shoulders – same as you. You went out in that and you can't swim?'

'That's different – I didn't have time to think about it. It was dark anyway. I couldn't see it.'

He looked up. Tom was standing above him in the sun, the water glistening on his face and chest and Storme was grinning down at him. 'That's brave,' she said. 'That's really brave. I wish you'd woken me up.'

'What?' said Tom. 'And terrified the calves out of their tiny little minds.'

Storme threw a punch at him, missed, and chased him away over the rise of the hill.

George clambered after them. A great weight seemed to have been removed. George was ashamed of his fears; most of them he managed to hide, but swimming was so open. Everyone else could do it – everyone else wanted to do it – even kids of six and seven back at the Home. And now for some reason he'd told Tom and Storme and they didn't mind. Better than that, Storme had called him 'brave'.

'Hurry up, George. Over here. Tea's up.' It was Storme, breaking in on his thoughts.

Tea was a biscuit. Tom was sunbathing on his back, chewing on a stalk of grass and George noticed that Tom had a proper chest, not like his own, which seemed to serve only as a link between his neck and his stomach. Tom was a little shorter than he was – that was something at least. Storme threw him a biscuit – the chocolate had melted.

'George?' said Tom, his eyes closed against the sun. 'Shall I teach you?'

'What?'

'To swim, ninny. I could teach you if you wanted.'
He propped himself up on one elbow. 'How about it?'

George looked at them both.

'Please,' said Storme.

'Is it deep in there?' he asked.

'Never out of your depth,' Tom said.

'When?'

'What's wrong with now?' said Tom.

They were both smiling at him. He was trapped, but he wanted to be.

'All right,' he said.

CHAPTER 5

GEORGE STOOD IN THE SHALLOWS, THE WATER freezing around his ankles, and watched Tom and Storme sliding in and out of the water like otters. The rocks were slippery under his feet and they turned to pebbles as he stepped forward gingerly. Tom and Storme were watching him; he couldn't turn back now. At every step his breath hissed back through his teeth; but now he was in and it wasn't worth getting out any more.

'Is it always this cold?' he asked, wading forward towards them holding his arms out like a tightrope walker.

'Always,' said Tom. 'The fish like it that way.'

The lesson lasted nearly a quarter of an hour – pushing off the rocks, walking races, lying back in the water – and by that time George was shivering as if he'd never stop. He staggered up the rocks into the drying warmth of the sun. He was pleased with himself. For the first time in his life he had taken his feet off the ground intentionally and felt the water carry him for a few brief seconds. He had felt the buoyancy of his body in the water. In the walking races from bank to bank he had enjoyed fighting the strength of the water with his arms – even if he had come in last each time.

They lay in the sun and baked. Storme was never quite sure of dragonflies; they looked beautiful and they never seemed to come too close, but there was something about them that made her wary – perhaps it was the name. A light-blue one hovered above her now, flitting against the glare of the sun. Storme stood up and shouted at it, but it didn't seem to be listening, so she flicked at it with her towel.

'What about the stone ring now?' she said. 'You've had your swim.'

Tom turned over to roast his back.

'How far is it?' said George.

'Not far.' Storme was eager. 'It's not far.'

'You can go if you like,' Tom muttered into the grass. 'I'm not moving an inch, too hot.'

He looked up at George.

'I warn you, it's just a few old stones and a heap of sheep's muck,' he said.

'All right,' said George, getting to his feet, 'long as it's not too far.'

'Nothing much to see,' Tom went on, 'and what there is is smelly.'

'Come on,' Storme said, tugging at George's arm. 'Don't listen to him. Let him go back to sleep.'

The going was hard, and George was already beginning to regret it. They crossed a stream and from then on it was uphill all the way. The sun disappeared behind a curtain of dull white cloud and the heat closed in around them.

Storme led the way, talking to George over her shoulder. 'Won't be long now. You all right?'

'I'm fine,' said George, wishing he was back with Tom lazing on the river bank.

Storme prattled on happily about the stone circles, about this, about that, and the clouds settled on the moor above them. The hilltops were hidden already.

Neither of them noticed. They were too busy negotiating rocks and gorsebushes.

There was a sudden cold about them, and the air was chill and damp. He looked up and then back down into the valley. There was no valley behind him and the hill above him was shrouded in mist. 'Storme,' he called out. 'Look! Up there!'

But Storme had seen it already. 'It's all around us.' Her voice was different; there was no echo. 'It's every-where.' Storme looked up to see if she could see the stone ring higher up the hillside, but the hill had vanished. It was like a bad dream just before you wake up – on every side a swirling white cloud was closing in on her – but there was no waking up, it was real. She ran down the hill to be closer to George. 'He said you should stay where you are,' she panted.

'Who did?' George was peering into the mist, looking for a clump of bushes he had passed just a few minutes before.

'Tom said. Dad as well – he's always going on about it. He says you must stay where you are. He says if you try to find your way off the moor in a mist you always get lost.'

'It's getting worse,' said George, thinking aloud.

'What are we going to do?' Storme could not disguise the fear in her voice.

George's mind was a muddle of instructions he'd received the last time he'd been out on the moor; he kept listing them and wondering if there were any he'd left out: don't wander around in a mist (Storme had confirmed that one); keep out of the wind; try to find shelter; keep warm; never go out on the moor without . . . he couldn't remember the details. And then he remembered the talk that the bearded man in the red anorak had given at the start of that Adventure Training course, about the mists on Dartmoor, about how quickly they come down winter or summer and that they could last for days . . .

'What are we going to do?' Storme was looking up at him. It had all been so quick. Minutes before they had been climbing up a sunny hillside toward Storme's stone circle.

'How far is it to your stone circle?' he asked.

'Almost there. I can't see it, but I know we're almost there. We must be.'

'At least there'll be some shelter there,' said George. 'Come on, we'll try for it.'

He found a track and kept to it, but as they climbed

the visibility worsened. Storme's hand crept into his and gripped it. George shivered. The heat of the day had vanished with the sun. He looked everywhere for the stones. There was only mist.

'The stones, are they big?' he said.

'Not really.'

'Right or left of the path?'

'Left . . . I think.' Storme's self-confidence was seeping away. The mist distorted everything. She could see nothing she could recognise. 'I'm not sure. I can't remember.'

George's voice seemed soft in the stillness. 'I'll look right, you look left. We'll go more slowly.' He squeezed her hand. 'We'll find it. Don't worry.'

It was George who spotted it first, a curve of grey in the mist. 'That it?' he said, and Storme ran past him whooping.

'We've found it, we've found it! Come on, there's a better one further up.'

He heard a cry ahead of him, and for a moment she disappeared. 'Storme? You all right?' He stopped and listened. There was crying ahead of him. He came on her suddenly – she was lying by the track. He bent over her, not knowing what to touch first.

'What happened?'

She grasped his hand. 'It's my ankle.' Her face was screwed up with pain.

'Are we close to the circle?'

'Behind me. I was turning when I saw it. My foot, I can't move it.'

George stood up and looked. There was the stone circle, smaller than he had imagined. 'Put your arms round my neck,' he said. 'I can carry you that far.' He pushed his hands underneath her and lifted her.

The wall of stones was low enough to clamber over. He swung her over and set her down gently on to one foot then jumped over after her.

'We got here,' he said, looking around. 'Tom was right, you know, it is a bit smelly.' Storme laughed a little through her crying and George helped her sit down by the wall. She stretched her leg out carefully, letting the ankle down slowly on to the ground. Her foot throbbed on the end of her leg and there was a knot of pain in between.

George was kneeling beside her. 'Can you move it?'

She shook her head. She didn't even bother to try; she knew she couldn't.

* * *

The dark was strangely comforting. It came on gradually, smothering through the swirling mist until there was only the damp and the musty smell to remind them the mist was still out there in the darkness. George scanned the gathering dark about him, looking, hoping for something, anything. Tom would be looking for them. Any moment he could come looming up out of the darkness and help them home.

They tried shouting out, just in case he was out there – first one by one and then together. 'Over here! We're here!' But the darkness seemed to soak up their words – there was no echo, no resonance, no matter how loud they shouted. It was futile and George knew it, but Storme insisted. 'He'll hear us,' she said. 'He's got to hear us.' But each time when the silence came back at them out of the gloom, Storme's voice became more desperate and more frightened. The dense black of night brought an end to any hope of early rescue. Now they knew they had to sit out the night, there was no choice; and as this became apparent they both accustomed themselves to the idea and stopped hoping against it.

They could not have been less well equipped to spend a night out on the moor. Dressed only in jeans and shirts, with no food, no water, they had no way of making a fire to counter the damp and the cold that was creeping into them.

As long as she didn't move it, Storme's ankle gave her little or no pain – the colder it got, the less it hurt – but every five or ten minutes, George made her stand up and perform violent physical exercises with her three good limbs; and he himself went through all the exercises he could remember from PE at school to bring some warmth back to his body. For a few minutes afterwards they felt better, but then the cold would set in once more and George would pull her to her feet again for another warm-up.

George couldn't think of any other way to keep warm; and he knew they had to keep warm, he'd learnt that much. He thought of building some kind of shelter up against the wall, but all he could come up with was two twigs, a sheep's skull and some feathers – and he didn't dare leave the stone ring to look for branches in case he couldn't find his way back again. But Storme couldn't go on with the exercises indefinitely. She was already exhausted and the cold was winning all the time. He felt it himself; he ached all over except where he could feel nothing. His hands and feet had long since lost any sensation, no matter how hard he stamped and clapped.

He peered down at Storme, who lay curled up like a baby with her back against the wall. She was looking at him. 'We will be all right, won't we?' she said, pushing herself up on to her elbows.

George tried to sound confident. 'Mist usually goes with the sun in the morning, doesn't it?' He crouched down beside her. 'All we have to do is to last out a few hours – four or five now, at the most. We'll be all right.'

'I was in bed last winter with 'flu. There was a mist outside the window for nearly the whole week.'

'That was the winter. It's summer now. All we've got to do is to keep warm until the morning. Come on, let's go for a walk.'

'Not again, George, please.'

'Come on,' he said.

He pulled her to her feet, put an arm round her, under her shoulder, and they set off, round and round until the feeling returned to his toes and they began to hurt again. Storme hopped along on one foot beside him, clinging on to him. Her leg was numb now – she tried to put some weight on her ankle and felt it give, but there was no pain.

'Can't feel my ankle,' said Storme. 'Can't feel much really. I wonder if that's what it's like when you die.'

'Don't know, never done it,' said George. 'Don't know, but we're going on walking until we get warmer. Faster now – hold tight, pegleg.' He felt her laughing against him.

'It feels like I haven't got a leg at all,' she said. 'It's funny. I can see it's there, but I can't feel a thing.'

George felt his shirt clinging cold to his back. He looked up into the sky for any glimmer of light that could be dawn; but it was too early and he knew it. Storme was coughing beside him, and leaning heavily against him. She could not go on walking for much longer. He found what little shelter there was up against the stone walls and they lay down side by side, huddled together against the wet and the cold. George looked up into the black above him and wondered what Tom was doing, whether he was looking for them or whether he had gone back for help.

'George,' Storme said quietly. 'I hope you stay with us.'

'So do I,' he said. 'Try to get some sleep. We've got to get all the way home in the morning.'

'We will get home, won't we?'

'Course,' he said. Storme was breathing regularly into his neck; it warmed the back of his ear. He shut his eyes and hoped he would sleep.

CHAPTER 6

'AT LEAST WE KNOW WHERE THEY ARE,' TOM'S mother said in an effort to cool the situation. 'And it's not too cold.'

'I couldn't have gone up after them, Dad,' Tom went on. 'I've only been up to that stone ring once. I'd never have found it in that mist.'

His father would not even look at him.

'You always told me never to move around if I was caught in a mist.'

His father turned on him. 'I've told you, haven't I? Haven't I told you time and time again – never to leave Storme alone out there.'

'She's not alone, she's with George.'

'And what does he know about the moor?'

'He's been up there before – he'll manage. He's not a fool, you know.'

Tom could feel the anger building up inside him. He'd had enough of his father's anger and his mother's quiet disapproval.

'And how many times have I told you to take the safety haversack with you up there?' his father went on. 'It's always the same, isn't it? You always know best. Sunny days, why bother? You didn't even tell us where you were going, you let Storme wander off as good as on her own . . .'

'But at least we know where they are – that's the main thing,' said Tom's mother, zipping up her anorak, 'and these summer mists don't usually last long, do they?'

'Do we?' Tom's father banged the table. 'Do we? Do we know where they are? Of course we don't. We know where they're heading for, but we don't know if they got there, do we? We don't know if they're still wandering around in circles out there. We don't know anything.'

'She wouldn't do that,' Tom said quietly.

Tom got no reply. He felt exhausted and battered. It

seemed hours ago now since he'd first realised something was wrong. It was the cold that had woken him up. The mist was blanketing the hills – it was the first thing he saw. The danger to Storme and George was obvious. He called for them, shouting up towards the hills. He crossed the stream and ran up into the mist on the other side shouting all the time, stopping every now and then to listen for a reply. None came. His instinct told him to follow the track, but the mist was thicker higher up and worsening all the time. He knew how easy it was to get lost in it. He turned and splashed back across the stream, up over the moor towards home, not stopping until he reached the barn by the house. There he paused to think how he would explain what had happened.

He felt his mother's hand on his shoulder. 'They'll be all right this time of year – bit wet and cold maybe, but they'll be all right. Come on, dear, drink your tea quickly – the sooner we get out there, the better.'

Tom had a cup of tea and a biscuit while his father checked the local weather forecast and his mother found the torches. His father put the phone down.

'What do they say?' Tom asked.

'Patchy – it'll be clear by the morning in most places.'

Tom drained his tea and thought of Storme and George. He wondered if they'd been talking about him, if they blamed him for letting them go off without him. Perhaps they had made it back to the river bank to find him gone. What would they think of him then?

'Come on, Tom,' said his father. 'Stop your dreaming, those two will be wondering where we've got to. I just hope they've been sensible, that's all.' There was a note of reconciliation in his voice. He felt he'd been hard on Tom, too hard probably, but he could not abide it when Tom tried to justify his mistakes; it reminded him of himself too much.

Tom closed the door behind them and the three of them stepped out into the swirling mist.

George couldn't sleep. He'd tried every position several times over, but each one lasted only a few minutes as the cold and the cramp crept into his legs and arms. Next to him Storme slept on, her slow, rhythmic breathing a constant reminder to him that he could not sleep. Once or twice he felt his eyes becoming heavy and forgot his discomfort, but always something jerked him back to consciousness.

He decided it was his head that was the trouble – there was nowhere to put it. The ground was too cold and the stones too hard. At one stage he tried to sleep sitting up. He'd seen people do that in films, on stagecoaches in particular, but as soon as he sat up he felt the wind on his face and the cold of his shirt against his body – so that didn't work either.

So he gave up the struggle for sleep, detached himself as gently as possible from Storme and clambered to his feet. He walked across the floor of the stone circle and looked out over the wall. There was no doubt about it – visibility was better, he could see that much further. The night seemed lighter, although he could still smell the mist in his nostrils when he breathed and could see it merging with the night further down the hillside. There was no doubt that it was lifting. He suppressed the shout of relief that came to his throat, and looked back across the stone circle to where Storme lay huddled up against the wall and he remembered that earlier they hadn't even been able to see the other side of the circle. He was considering whether to wake her and tell her the good news, whether it was worth trying to get home in the dark, when he heard the voices.

At first he could not take it in. He had become so used to the dull silence of the moor and the deadening mist that the sound seemed unreal, even ghostly. He stopped breathing and listened again until he was sure he could believe his ears. It *was* voices and they were coming from the darkness at the foot of the hillside. He felt his heart pumping in his ears.

'Up here! We're up here! Up here!' His voice was cracking. For an instant there was no reply and he wondered if he might have been imagining things. But there had been voices – there had been.

'George?' It was Tom's voice. 'George! Where are you?'

'Here! Up here!' George was laughing now. He could see lights. He jumped up on to the wall. 'Keep coming, you can't miss us.'

Storme was behind him; he helped her up. 'Is it them?' she cried. 'Is it them?'

'Hope so,' said George, helping her to balance beside him on the stones. 'Look!' There were three dull lights dancing up the hill towards them. There was no beam, just three small dancing circles of light.

'Stay where you are!' It was Mr Dyer's voice. 'We'll be right there.'

The lights turned to torch beams, the voices to dark shapes and the shapes to people. Tom was first over the wall.

'You all right?' Tom said.

'Bit cold,' said George.

'Nice place you got here.' Tom shone his torch round the stone circle. The two boys laughed together, Tom with relief that they were safe and that George seemed pleased to see him, and George with relief that the cold vigil was at last over.

Storme was hugging everyone except Tom, who avoided her clutches. Her father was for turning round immediately and getting home before the mist changed its mind and came down again, cutting them off from home, but her mother was pouring out the hot tea she'd brought in a thermos and seeing to Storme's ankle.

'It's puffy,' she said, pressing it gently. 'You mustn't put any weight on it on the way back. We'll have to help you.'

'George can do it,' said Storme. 'Can't you, George?' George felt the warmth of the tea spreading through his body in delicious waves.

'He won't be able to manage you on his own,' said Mrs Dyer, helping Storme into a dry jumper and her anorak. 'We'll do one on each arm. It's a long walk, over two hours it took us.'

The way back was slow and long. In places the mist still hovered, threatening. Mr Dyer led the way, shouting occasional warnings over his shoulder about rabbit holes and rocks in the track. But it was Storme's ankle that slowed them down. To start with she managed well enough with one arm round George's neck and the other round her mother's, but as she warmed up under her anorak, the pain in her ankle intensified. She kept it well above the ground, but even so every step she took with her good leg jarred the ankle; even George's words of encouragement fell on deaf ears as her mind became more and more absorbed with the dread of the next step.

They stopped frequently in an effort to ease her pain; a bandage from the safety haversack seemed to provide temporary relief – but it was only temporary.

She tried to fight the pain but it was too much for her; she cried involuntarily. There was nothing else for it – they had to carry her.

They took it in turns after that, Storme clinging on round their necks. But she was heavy, and no one could carry her for long, not even Mr Dyer. All the while Storme tried to stop herself from crying out loud. She longed for her warm bed and for her ankle to stop throbbing.

Tom set her down to rest his aching arms.

'I'll do the rest – it's not far,' said his mother. 'I haven't carried her yet. Come on, Storme, my turn. Arms round my neck, there's a good girl.'

Tom watched them walk slowly down the hill and waited for George to join him. George was beginning to feel the effects of a night without sleep. He found he had very little strength in his legs. He was tiring fast, often stumbling over tussocks or molehills. Tom grabbed his arm to help him. George turned and smiled wearily at him. Then he saw the farm below them on the far side of the river. His legs found new strength, and he stepped out eagerly now towards home and a warm bed.

*　*　*

Storme liked Dr Hendie; he was always joking and laughing. He'd often sit and chat on the side of the bed, puffing clouds of smoke out of his pipe. Tom showed him in; that was strange. Usually it was Mum who brought him in.

'Let's have a look at it, then,' Dr Hendie said. There was no pipe, no chat. His hands felt cold on her ankle. 'Wiggle your toes,' the doctor said, speaking to her foot rather than to her. She wiggled her toes – there was no real pain. 'It's a sprain. You'll survive, this time.' He was looking at her now and he was not pleased. 'I heard about last night – your brother told me. You were lucky, very lucky.'

He bandaged the ankle in silence, as if it didn't belong to her. Storme couldn't think of anything to say – he'd never been as frosty as this before. He tested her chest with his cold stethoscope and tapped her back. He clipped his bag shut and stood up. 'You'll stay in your bed for a day or so.'

He stopped by the door on the way out. 'Storme?'

'Yes?'

'I've been a doctor here for thirty years now and I've examined several children who got lost up on the moor. Some of them were dead – no second chance for them. Don't you ever wander off like that again, understand?'

Storme nodded. There was no cheery goodbye, no chin-chucking or tickling and Storme was left staring at her closed door. She could hear talking outside – her father's voice and Dr Hendie's – but they were talking too low for her to hear what they were saying.

The door opened. It was Tom. George came in behind him. They kept looking at each other.

'Not broken then,' Tom said.

'Sprain, he said.' Storme smiled at George. 'But I've got to stay in bed for a bit.' She leaned forward. 'What's the matter with the doctor, anyway?' she whispered.

'It's Mum,' said Tom. Storme looked at him sharply. There was something wrong; she could always tell when Tom was upset, his voice went quiet and he couldn't look at you.

'What's the matter with her?'

'The doctor's in with her now,' Tom said.

'What's the matter?' Storme looked from one to the other.

'It's her back. She can't move – she can't sit up or walk or anything. He's called an ambulance.'

'An ambulance! But she was all right. She put me to bed. She even carried me up here, I remember. There was nothing wrong with her.'

'She carried you upstairs as well?' George said, and he looked across the bed at Tom.

'It must have been that then,' said Tom.

'What?' Storme felt her voice rising.

'Dad says she had an accident, years ago, a fall, and she did something to her back, a disc I think he said. She was in hospital a long time, before they were married it was. Dr Hendie looked after her then. There's never been any trouble since – not in over twenty years. The doctor asked Dad if she'd been lifting anything heavy.' Tom looked at Storme. She understood now – there was no need to go on.

Tom was expecting her to cry and waited for the tears to come, but they didn't. Perhaps she felt numb like he had when he'd been up to see his mother in her bedroom. The radio had been on and she was lying out straight, so that all he could see was a tuft of grey-black hair on her pillow. Tom saw that she'd been crying; the only colour left in her face was the red round her eyes. She smiled weakly at him and turned her face away.

'She'll be all right though. The doctor said so,' Tom said.

'Can I see her?' Storme said.

'Dr Hendie gave her something, a pain-killer. She's asleep, and anyway the ambulance'll be here soon.'

'Hospital?' she said. 'She's going into hospital?'

'She's going to Exeter,' said Tom. And then Storme cried, and there was nothing Tom or George could say that would comfort her.

They heard the ambulance draw up outside. There were voices outside the window and the sound of feet on the gravel. They heard the front door open and steps on the stairs. Tom pushed open the window and George helped Storme out of bed and across the room. She hobbled slowly but was in time to see the stretcher come out of the house and disappear into the ambulance. The doors closed after it.

Dr Hendie walked slowly towards his car with Mr Dyer. Tom strained his ears to hear what they were saying, but the ambulance revved up and moved off, obliterating their words. Dr Hendie said no goodbye to his father. He just got into his car and slammed the door.

They stood by the window watching the ambulance

rocking slowly from side to side up the drive-way over the cattle grid and on to the road. Dr Hendie's little green car was almost hidden in the dust behind it. They watched in silence until they could no longer see the white roof of the ambulance.

'She's never been away before – she's always been here,' Storme said quietly.

CHAPTER 7

TIME WAS OUT OF ORDER ALL THAT DAY AND THE house had gone quiet. Tom's father had hardly spoken since the ambulance had driven away. At tea, which was a mixture of all the meals they'd missed – corn flakes and pork pies – George kept searching for the right thing to say to Tom, but he could never find the words, so he said nothing. Tea without Mrs Dyer was a solemn affair. George waited for Tom or his father to say something to cover the rattle and scrape of knives and forks, but nothing beyond, 'Pass the milk,' or, 'Baked beans please,' was said. He was greatly relieved when Mr Dyer asked him to put Storme's food on a tray and take it upstairs to her.

Storme was propped up in bed and waiting for him to come in. He nudged the door further open. ' 'Bout time,' she said, patting at the sheets on her lap. 'No one's been up here all afternoon. What've you all been doing?'

'Outside with your dad.'

'What, all afternoon?'

'Moving sacks most of the time.'

Storme jogged the tray as she sat up and her orange juice splashed over her pork pie. 'Oh God,' she groaned. George wiped the pork pie dry and gave it back to her. She smiled at him; it was the first smile he'd seen all day.

'How's your ankle?' he said as Storme bit into her pie.

'Better I think. Haven't tried it out since this morning when Mum went. Anything about Mum yet?'

'Your dad said he'd phone later this evening. You mustn't worry about her, Storme – she'll be all right.'

'It was our fault, wasn't it?' she said, looking down at her plate. 'If we hadn't gone up to the stone circle it would never have happened – she wouldn't be in hospital.' Her voice softened and George saw that she was crying quietly, keeping her face away from him. It upset him, but he preferred it to the sullen, controlled sadness of downstairs.

'It's not your fault, Storme – you didn't make the mist come down, did you? It was luck, that's all, just bad luck.' He moved the tray off the bed and on to the floor, and Storme pushed herself down the bed and turned her head into the pillow. George didn't say any more, but patted her shoulder gently.

There was a car starting up outside the window, and by the time he got there Mr Dyer's car was bumping up the drive leaving the chickens in the yard flapping their wings and squawking angrily.

The door opened and Tom came in quietly. 'Is she asleep?' he whispered, pointing at the bed.

'No, I'm not,' Storme mumbled into her pillow.

'Where's he gone?' George asked.

'Gran and Grandpa's, up the road. He wants to tell them about Mum – didn't want to do it on the phone.'

Tom saw the tray on the floor. 'You've hardly touched it, Storme.'

'I don't want it,' Storme muttered.

George was watching her to see if she was still crying, but her voice was firmer, her shoulders were still; she was just hiding her face, giving herself time. He smiled to himself, understanding her.

Tom sat on the end of the bed; he looked serious.

'Mind my foot!' Storme shouted, lifting her face from the pillow for an instant.

No one said anything for a moment or two, but George could see Tom was about to say something – he was fidgeting nervously, picking at his nails.

Tom spoke without looking up. 'I had a row with Dad – after Mum went.'

'What about?' George asked.

'Nothing new in that – you're always on at each other.' Storme seemed to be feeling better already.

Tom ignored her. 'He said that Mum probably wouldn't be back for weeks.' He spoke hesitantly.

'But why the row?' George felt he was hiding something.

'He said that if Mum is away that long he couldn't manage the farm and us and he'd have to see if Gran and Grandpa could have us up with them till school starts.'

Storme was sitting up now; she looked alarmed and George could not understand why. He still didn't see the need for a row.

'But we can't go there,' said Storme. 'They've only got one spare room, and it's tiny.'

'That's what I said,' Tom went on, 'and he said that George might have to go back.' He paused for a moment and looked up at George. 'He didn't think they could be expected to look after George as well as us.'

'Well, what did you say?' Storme said and she saw that George had turned away and was looking out of the window.

'I said we wouldn't go.'

'I won't go,' Storme shouted. 'I won't go. It's not fair. We can stay here. Why can't we stay here?' Her voice rose until it wavered and George hoped she wouldn't cry again.

It had not crossed his mind that he would ever have to leave; he simply had not considered the possibility. He thought of the bedroom he shared at the Home, that high, empty dining-room, and the wall he sat on under the trees by the front gate. Up to now it had been home and he had looked forward to getting back there, but now the thought of that emptiness, of being alone again, filled him with dread.

'We won't let you go back,' Tom was close behind

him – it was as if he could read his mind. 'And anyway, Dad said he'd think about it. It'll be all right.'

'It had better be,' said Storme. 'It was Mum that wanted George to come. I'll tell her. She wouldn't let Dad do it.'

'No,' said Tom. 'Mum's in bad enough trouble without this as well. We mustn't say anything to her about it.'

'When are we going to see her, anyway?'

'Dad's ringing the hospital later this evening to find out how she is. If everything's all right, we'll go over on Saturday afternoon.'

'That's ages,' Storme said. 'Why can't we go tomorrow?'

'Visiting time's the same time as milking time. Dad says he could get Jo to come in on Saturdays. We can't leave the farm. Won't run by itself,' Tom said, imitating his father's gruffness. 'It's only three days away anyway, and I don't suppose she'll want to see anyone for a day or so – you don't when you're feeling that rotten.'

George had been trying to keep his mind on what they were saying, but no matter how hard he tried he could not forget the threat that now hung over him;

he was weighing up the chances of his being sent back.

'Did you say he's gone off to see your grandparents now, in the car?'

Tom nodded.

'They'll be deciding about me won't they?' He didn't wait for Tom's answer; he knew it already. 'What are they like, your grandparents?'

'They won't mind having you,' said Storme. 'They'll understand. Grandpa'll understand – he's really nice. He'll understand.'

'But what about her?' Tom said. 'She's as fussy as they come. Everything has to be just right: slippers by the front door, tea cosies and tiptoe. She'll never agree to having three of us in that one room.'

'But what about Grandpa . . .'

'Grandpa does what he's told. He'll do anything that Gran asks. It's not up to him, it's up to her, and if Dad asks them she'll say no.'

'So that's that then,' George said.

'No it's not,' said Tom firmly. 'I told you, you're staying here. I'll keep on at Dad – it's the only way with him. I'll try to persuade him we can stay here and look after ourselves.'

'And what if you can't?' Storme challenged him.

'I don't know, I don't know – but let's try it anyway. It's the only hope. And you never know, Gran may not want to have any of us. She doesn't like me much, my hair's too long.'

Tom tried to sound optimistic, but he knew his father well enough. He knew he could never cope with the unexpected. However helpful the three of them were, however hard they tried, he knew his father had made up his mind that he could not run the farm and look after them at the same time. His father was never the kind of person who had his mind changed easily unless Mum was around to do it tactfully for him, so gently that he hardly noticed.

He caught George's eye for a moment. 'It'll work out,' he said, 'you'll see.' It sounded unconvincing even to him.

Mr Dyer came back later that evening to find Tom and George mending a fence and Storme hobbling about in her dressing-gown doing the washing-up. For the next three days they set out to prove they could manage. Every morning they were up at dawn, before Mr Dyer, to do the milking and the feeding, while Storme took control in the kitchen. Her ankle still troubled her, but she had worked out a limp that minimised the weight on her bad leg. Neither Tom nor Storme mentioned their grandparents again, or even the possibility that George might have to leave. They did everything they could not to antagonise their father.

George tried to avoid Mr Dyer as much as possible. He felt hurt and resentful that Mr Dyer's first reaction to the new situation was to suggest that he was somehow in the way and expendable, and he found it difficult to hide his feelings so he spent all his time with either Tom or Storme as a kind of insurance against having to talk to Mr Dyer alone.

The news from the hospital in Exeter was the same each evening. She was comfortable, or as comfortable as could be expected. No, they didn't yet know whether there would have to be an operation; and yes, visiting hours on Saturdays were from two to five in the afternoon. The phone calls seemed to drive Mr Dyer into a deeper state of gloom. He was irritated by Storme's questions and seemed oblivious to everything they were doing to help.

But Tom was feeling more confident already. Between them they were running the farm and the house with great success. There had been no great mishaps, although his father had complained once that the food was mostly out of tins; but on the whole Storme's cooking was edible enough and she did keep a tidy kitchen. Each day Tom thought his father seemed easier and more relaxed until the evening phone calls, first the one to the hospital and then the one to Gran's.

He decided to tackle his father about George on the Saturday morning before they left for the hospital. That gave them as long as possible to prove their point and it also put off the confrontation that he was dreading. If his father had already made up his mind, arguing with him would just make him more obstinate. But he had to try, he'd promised George. He could never argue with his father without losing his temper, and losing his temper meant losing the argument. The gentle persuasion of the last few days was the only chance, and he knew it.

After the phone calls on Friday evening, Storme was making cocoa in the kitchen. Dad always liked a cup of cocoa in the evening after his tea and it helped to cheer him up after the phone calls. The cocoa was in the larder, on the bottom shelf behind the sugar.

With the tin in her hand she climbed the two steps back up into the kitchen. She saw the white froth of the boiling milk creeping up over the rim of the saucepan on the range. She forgot her ankle and took the last step too quickly; her foot caught the edge of the step; she felt herself falling and threw out her other leg to balance herself; her ankle gave and twisted under her. She heard herself crying out somewhere in the distance. The cocoa tin crashed to the floor. She was looking up. Tom was there with George and behind them she could see the milk boiling over on to the range and the smoke rising into the air. There was a sharp pain in the side of her head. She heard her father's voice and recognised the smell of rice-pudding skin. The milk's boiled over, she thought.

It took all three of them to carry her upstairs; George went on ahead opening the doors. Storme kept insisting she could walk and that she didn't need to be carried, but they carried her in spite of it. She couldn't decide which was worse, the pain in her head, the nausea that was creeping up from her stomach or the heavy throb in her ankle. She nearly cried out when her ankle got caught between the bannister rail and the wall as her father reached the top of the stairs. Once in her bed, though, it was the sickness that took over; she put her head back on the pillow and prayed that the sweet taste in her mouth didn't mean she was going to be sick. But it did. She thought it would never stop, and when it had finished, her head and her ankle throbbed in perfect unison. She lay back again. George was there, talking to her and she felt the cool relief of a cold flannel around her ankle. She opened her eyes to thank him. Tom and her father had gone.

'Is that better?' George was asking. Storme nodded. 'All for a cup of cocoa,' he said.

Storme pushed herself up on to her elbows and felt her head, looking for the bump; she found it where she expected to, just above her ear.

'You hit your head on the stove. It looked as if you'd made a dive for the saucepan. You must have been knocked out for a few seconds – when we came . . .'

'Sssssh!' Storme hissed. 'Listen!' She was pointing down through the floorboards. It was Mr Dyer's voice and he was angry.

'That's it. That's final!' he was saying. 'I told you, didn't I? I said she should stay in bed, like Dr Hendie said. But oh no, she could get up to help in the kitchen, it would be all right, you'd manage everything. Don't worry, Dad, you said, we can cope on our own – you don't need to worry about us. Only a few days ago you wanted nothing to do with him, remember? I told you Gran and Grandpa would be pleased to have you with them, but that wouldn't do unless George could go with you. I even asked them. Do you know that? I asked them whether George could camp down on their sitting-room floor. As if I haven't got enough on my mind as it is.'

Tom had been listening long enough. 'We asked him here, didn't we? He didn't ask to come here. We asked him. Mum said until the end of our holidays – that's still over three weeks away – and he's been here less than a week. You can't just wrap him up and pack him off like a parcel just because it's a bit inconvenient. He likes it here. I like having him and so does Storme.'

'And what has that got to do with it? Your mother's in hospital, Storme's in bed – largely because you had to prove you were right. Well, you were wrong. You can't run this place. It didn't work.'

He sat down at the table and Tom noticed he had stopped shouting – his voice was lower, more considerate. 'You tried, Tom. I know that, I'm not blind – and you know I've nothing against George personally. He's a good lad and I'm not forgetting what he's done for us since he's been here. I watched you all – you worked hard, all three of you, I'll not deny that. But now look – we have to run the farm at about the busiest time of year, feed ourselves, look after the house and look after Storme. We just can't do it.' He paused and looked up at Tom. 'I know how you feel about George. But we can always have him back some other time – when Mum's better.'

Tom sat down opposite him. 'But, Dad, listen. We can manage – I know we can. I know Mum would want us to try.' It was a bad move and Tom knew it as he spoke.

'Don't tell me what your mother would want.' He stood up again and Tom heard the anger back in his voice. 'I think I should know that better than you. Anyway, it's no good your going on about it, I've made up my mind. I've asked Gran and she's happy to have the two of you. I'll ring up Mrs Thomas now and ask her to fetch George as soon as she can.' He walked towards the door.

'Dad,' Tom said quietly. 'I told you last time. We

won't go, and George isn't going anywhere.'

'You'll do as you're told,' said his father. 'You'll do just what you're told.' The kitchen door slammed behind him and Tom heard the ping of the telephone in the hall.

There had never been any need to challenge his father quite like this. His mother had always been there to find a compromise, to mediate and to help him sidestep any direct confrontation. Now there was no room any more for compromise and no one to help achieve it. He felt angry with himself at his failure to persuade his father, and angry with his father at his insensitive inflexibility. He would not let George be driven away. He wanted him to stay. He would not let it happen.

George and Storme had heard every word through the floorboards, and as soon as Storme heard the door slam downstairs she sent George to the door to listen. He opened the door, turning the handle gently and releasing it slowly.

'All right, Mrs Thomas. Sunday afternoon – yes, and I'll be able to tell you more then . . . sorry? . . . Yes, I will, I'll tell her when I see her tomorrow . . . right. 'Bye.'

It was done. George closed the door silently and looked at Storme, who was sitting on the end of her bed.

'Sunday,' he said. 'She's coming to fetch me on Sunday.'

CHAPER 8

THE JOURNEY TO THE HOSPITAL HAD BEEN MADE in total silence. Mr Dyer parked the car. He felt he had to say something. 'There's no other way,' he said. 'You know that, don't you, George? There's nothing else I can do. You understand, don't you, George?'

George was still thinking how to reply when Tom spoke up. 'Of course he understands, he understands only too well. He understands that this time tomorrow he'll be back where he came from. Storme wants him to stay, I want him to stay and you know Mum would want him . . .'

'You leave your mother out of this,' his father

snapped at him. 'I told you to leave her out of it. I don't want her all worried about this. She's not to hear of it, not a word, you understand?'

Mr Dyer caught Storme's eye and looked away. Once or twice on the way to the hospital he'd caught her eye in the driving mirror and it was the same unblinking stare as before. He was used to her hysterics and her quick temper, but this defiant and silent hatred was new and he didn't know how to deal with it. She'd not said a word to him since the telephone call the day before. He glanced up at the mirror again. She was still looking at the back of his neck.

He shifted in his seat, swivelling round so that he could talk to all three of them in the back seat. He softened his voice, trying to conciliate now. 'Listen all of you. I told Tom yesterday. You can come back next summer, George, maybe even before that. Next holidays if Mum's better.' He paused, waiting for a response from George. Mr Dyer went on. 'Now come on – let's not look gloomy. If she sees you like this, she'll know something's up.'

He opened the car door as an ambulance roared past and into the hospital entrance, sirens blaring and lights flashing. Tom and George helped Storme out.

'See?' said Mr Dyer as they stood watching the ambulance unload. 'You see? There's always someone worse off than yourself.'

No one walked with him across the tarmac. He could sense their antagonism behind him. He could bear that. Tomorrow they'd all be gone and he could concentrate on the farm. The sheep had to be dipped in the next ten days, and that slow puncture on the tractor had to be mended before he could get the three calves to market by Wednesday. He wondered if the price of the calves had dropped yet again. He looked behind him to check that he wasn't too far in front of them. The three of them looked right together, the two boys supporting Storme on either side. He saw Storme look up at George and manage a smile. It was a pity, he thought, a pity to split them up, but it was the only thing he could do. Anyway they'd get over it – children always do.

George had a horror of hospitals. It was the camouflaging smells, the squeaky shoes on rubber floors, the lowered voices of white-coated doctors, the stretchers and the wheelchairs. To him it all suggested pain and death. Storme's fingers gripped his neck tighter. He looked down at her and then across at Tom who winked at him.

The car had been a silent nightmare for George. In the house they could avoid Mr Dyer, but the enforced proximity of the car seemed to intensify the bitterness. George didn't hate Mr Dyer; he just didn't understand why they couldn't all stay together. He found he couldn't look at Mr Dyer as Tom's father any more. He was the man who wanted him to be taken away. But his sadness at the prospect of leaving was lightened by Tom's efforts on his behalf, his confidence that things would somehow work out all right, and by Storme's obvious affection for him.

They followed Mr Dyer into the ward. Storme looked at the faces propped up on the pillows on either side of her. One had her mouth wide open in sleep. There were no teeth. She had never seen anyone who looked that old.

Her mother wasn't propped up in bed like the others; she was lying flat on her back smiling up at everyone. Tom bent over his mother and kissed her. Her cheek was hot. 'Feel that,' she said, grasping Tom's hand and putting it on her stomach. 'I'm well and truly mummified now,' she laughed. Storme leaned over from her chair and joined in the investigation, feeling up and down the bedclothes. 'Go on, right down to my knees, keep going,' her mother said, and she pushed back the blankets and knocked on her stomach through her crisp white hospital nightgown. It rang hollow. 'Plaster. Solid as a rock,' she grinned. 'I'll never get out of it!'

George had kept away from the family kissing-ritual, and was standing at the end of the bed. 'Come and feel it, George,' Mrs Dyer said, beckoning him to come closer. 'Has Storme taken you on any more walks?' Everyone was laughing again.

For a few brief moments as George watched, it was like it had been before the accident. Their pleasure at seeing her again, and her obvious joy at being with them all, seemed to remove the cloud that was threatening them. She joked on about her plaster cast – they called her 'the iron maiden' in the ward, she said. All the problems seemed suddenly forgotten. But George knew it could not last for long. Sooner or later she would start asking about them. It was sooner rather than later. How is everyone? How are you managing without me? The farm? The house? Storme's ankle? The smiles were wiped away as Mr

Dyer reassured her that all was well. He was very convincing.

Tom, Storme and George watched him from the other side of the bed as he painted a picture of domestic calm and sweet accord. At one point Tom heard Storme draw in her breath to interrupt, and he trod hard on her toe. It was her bad foot, but she stifled her pain and anger and looked away from her mother's bed until she regained her composure.

Then the questions became more direct, more personal – questions Mr Dyer had to think about carefully so that he could answer them without arousing her suspicions. Was Tom looking after George? Was George enjoying his stay? Who had been looking after her kitchen? What were they eating? They answered as briefly as possible, trying to avoid her eyes, but she kept on at them. 'Not much of a holiday for you, is it, George?' she said. 'But we'll put that right as soon as I get home, won't we, dear?' She glanced up at her husband who was looking anxiously at George, and Tom felt he saw a flicker of doubt in her eyes as she looked back to George. She changed the subject. 'The doctors say it's not nearly as bad as they thought. I've got two discs out of place, that's all.

I won't be more than two weeks in here, at the most, they said. Then we'll make it up to you. All right?'

George tried a smile and nodded. He was a bad actor. He felt her eyes still on his face and looked down at the end of the bed. Tom looked at his mother – he was sure she was aware that something was wrong, but the visiting bell sounded and there was a smiling nurse pacing the ward. 'Time gentlemen, please,' she said.

Mr Dyer stayed behind for a minute or so and then joined them outside the ward. No one said a thing on the way back to the car.

'Did you tell her?' Tom asked from the back of the car.

'No,' he said quietly.

'She knows anyway,' Tom said.

'Maybe,' said his father in such a way that meant he wasn't going to talk about it.

Next to Tom in the back seat, George wondered if he'd ever see Mrs Dyer again.

From Storme's window they watched for the first sign of Mrs Thomas's car. It had started to rain outside so that they had to peer between the streaks on the window. Lunch had been another silent affair, and George had eaten next to nothing. Mr Dyer had made them Welsh Rarebit with an egg on the top – Buck Rarebit, he called it. George pricked the yolk of his egg and tried to stop the yellow liquid from spilling over the edge of the toast and on to the plate. He tried one or two mouthfuls – chewing a long time on each one – but that was all he could manage. Even that he had to force himself to swallow, helping it down with gulps of water. For some minutes, while Tom and his father finished their meal, he played with the congealing egg yolk, watching it harden over the cheese. Then he could bear the silence no longer and left the room muttering something about fetching Storme's tray.

'Mrs Thomas'll be here shortly,' Mr Dyer said as he was going out. 'Are you all packed up?'

'Think so,' George said. He stopped outside the door to see if Tom would say anything to his father. Instead, he heard the clatter of a knife and fork on a plate, the noisy scraping of a chair and Tom joined him, still chewing. Tom took his elbow and ushered him upstairs, putting his finger to his lips. Once inside Storme's room they talked in whispers until they heard the kitchen door open and close, and Mr Dyer's footsteps heavy on the gravel outside.

'Mum meant what she said, George,' Tom said. 'I'm sure of that.'

'What do you mean?' George was trying to remember what it was that she'd said.

'She'll be out in less than two weeks,' said Tom, 'and she'll expect to find you here. She won't stand for it when she knows – she'll get you back.'

'But that'll be too late,' said George, 'almost the end of the holidays. I'm back at school at the beginning of September.'

'So are we,' Tom said and he threw a meaningful look at Storme who nodded back. 'George, we were thinking, Strome and me that is, we were thinking that maybe we'd ask Mum . . .'

'What?'

'Well, Storme thought you might like to come and live here.'

'What d'you mean?'

'She means permanently, full time, don't you, Storme?'

Storme was sitting up in bed, her eyes bright with excitement.

'It's not only me,' she said. 'Tom thought of it.'

Tom had moved off the bed and was standing by the window. George looked from one to the other still not believing what they were saying. He heard the tractor start up outside.

'But what about your dad? Have you asked him? And your mum, what will she say?'

'Haven't said anything yet,' said Tom.

'But we will,' Storme insisted, 'when she gets out. We'll ask her, I promise you. She'll say yes, I know she will.'

'She thinks the world of you, George,' said Tom. 'She'll be furious when she hears about this.' He dug his hands into his pockets. 'It's Dad who's the difficult one – not because he doesn't like you – he likes you a lot. I can tell that. But if he's made to feel guilty about sending you away, he'll never agree. I've seen him when he feels bad about something he's done – he can never admit it, he digs his heels in and he won't budge. You remember when he shot that dog, Storme, a couple of years ago? It was after the sheep. He was almost in tears after that, really upset he was; but then the man who owned the dog, Phil Oakes, I think it was, he came along and had a go at Dad, told him he was a callous brute, his dog had never touched any sheep. I remember, we listened from up here, didn't we, Storme? Real fireworks it was and I've never seen Dad so mad at anyone.'

'But you've hardly said a kind word to him for days now,' George said.

'I know, we've thought of that,' said Storme. 'We've thought of everything.'

Tom left the window. 'After you've gone – in fact as soon as Mrs Thomas gets here – the tactics change. No more dark looks, we'll be all smiles, won't we, Storme? Tomorrow morning we'll go off to Gran's without a murmur – we'll even look forward to going. Storme will be a good patient and I'll come back each day to help Dad out.' He paused and looked at George for his approval. 'Well? What do you think?'

'Bit sudden, isn't it?' said George, thinking aloud. 'I mean, won't he think it's odd?'

'Not if I explain. I'll tell him after a bit. I'll tell him we were angry and sad that you had to go – we liked you a lot, liked having you here, and just didn't want you to go – but now we realise he was right, we couldn't have managed on our own, you had to go

and isn't it good of Gran to look after us. Good, eh?'
Tom smiled.

'Tell him about Mum,' said Storme.

'I'm coming to that,' Tom said sharply. He didn't
like being rushed. 'I think she knows, about you going
I mean.'

'How do you know?' said George.

'I don't know, it's just a feeling. She knows something is odd and I think she knows it's about you – she
won't take long to work it out. Anyway I'm going to
see her. I'm getting the bus into Exeter on Tuesday
morning. I'll tell her everything that's happened.'

'I wish I could come,' said Storme.

'Don't start that again. We agreed, didn't we? You
stay and be nice to Gran and I'll ask Mum about
George.'

'How will I know what she says?' said George.

'I'll write and tell you – but I know it'll be all right.'

Tom tried to sound more confident than he really
was. It wouldn't be that easy. There was his father to
placate, his mother to persuade and the delicate
problem of playing one off against the other.

Storme reached out and squeezed George's hand.
'It'll work, you'll see,' she said.

'I hope you're right,' said George, and he squeezed her hand in response and joined Tom who was back by the window.

Storme got off the bed and hopped across the room after him and balanced herself against George's shoulder. 'It's raining,' she said.

'She'll be here any minute,' George said, looking through the rain and the trees towards the top of the farm track for the first glimpse of Mrs Thomas' battered blue Mini.

'You'll be back,' Tom said quietly and deliberately. 'I promise you'll be back.'

They didn't have long to wait, and once Mrs Thomas did arrive George had little time to think about what was happening. Within minutes he was sitting inside the car waiting for Mrs Thomas to finish her chat with Mr Dyer. Storme waved from her bedroom window whenever he looked up at her. Tom hovered round the car not knowing what to say, but smiling encouragement through the car window. George felt the awkwardness and wished Mrs Thomas would hurry up and drive him away. As if in answer, Mrs Thomas came running out of the house, her mac over her head. Mr Dyer stomped after her in his muddy boots. He leaned in the window after she'd got in.

'As I said, Mrs Thomas, he's been a good lad, no trouble at all. We'll have him back any time you like after my wife's better.' He looked across Mrs Thomas at George. 'I'm sorry, George, I really am; but you understand, don't you?'

George nodded and managed a smile.

Then Tom was banging on his window and waving his arms, mouthing like a goldfish. George rolled down the window. 'Your address – I haven't got your address,' he shouted. 'Can you wait a moment?' He dashed back indoors and reappeared moments later with a pencil and an old envelope. George dictated the address of the Home.

'That's a good idea,' said Mr Dyer. 'You can write to each other. Be good for Storme to write a letter or two, she needs the practice.'

George thought he detected a ghost of a smile on Tom's face as he finished writing, but it was gone by the time he looked up again.

Mrs Thomas had three tries at starting the engine. 'Third time lucky,' she said, as the car spluttered and coughed and then roared to life.

'All the best,' said Mr Dyer, standing back.

' 'Bye, George,' said Tom, looking hard at him. He smiled and winked and tapped the envelope.

' 'Bye,' said George, lifting his voice over the revving of the engine. He looked up and waved for a last time at Storme who had her nose pressed against the window; the rest of her face obscured by steam and rain. Mrs Thomas fought with the wheel and the car moved off up the track. She clicked a switch and the windscreen wipers hummed into rhythm. Then they were over the cattle grid and out on to the smooth surface of the tarmac road.

Mrs Thomas spoke for the first time. 'They weren't so bad after all, then.'

'No,' he said, reaching for the radio. 'Not too bad.'

CHAPTER 9

TO BE AWAY FROM THE FARM WAS HARD ENOUGH
in itself, but to be somewhere else was much worse.
George threw his suitcase on to his bed and sat down
beside it. He could hear Mrs Thomas downstairs. She
would be explaining what had happened to his housemother, Nancy. Nancy was laughing the same high-
pitched, nervous laugh that punctuated any conversation no matter how serious. It was almost always
followed by her dry smoker's cough, a sharp hacking
cough which was inevitably followed by 'Excuse *me*'.
George waited for the 'Excuse *me*' and then pushed the
door with his foot until it clicked shut. He was back.

He looked under Jimmy's pillow for his pyjamas;

they weren't there; he must still be away on holiday. That was something to be thankful for anyway; the thought of facing Jimmy's questions appalled him. Jimmy Tyler was his room-mate, had been for nearly two years now, off and on. He was eight when he first arrived, and no one seemed to like him much; that was why Nancy had put him in with George. 'You'll look after him,' she'd said, 'won't you, George? Jimmy, this is George, our eldest boy, he'll look after you.' Jimmy didn't say a word for months. He'd cried himself to sleep at nights and spent the day at school wandering about by himself, crying quietly. Then one day, sitting on that bed, he'd told George about his mother and father and how they'd gone out to the cinema one evening and never come back. Their car skidded off the by-pass – they were both dead. After he'd told him, Jimmy couldn't leave George alone and he followed him around like a loyal sheepdog. George felt sorry for him, but could never learn to like him. He picked his nose, his feet smelt in the evening and he kept breaking George's things, 'by accident'.

Outside it was still raining, but George could just make out the clock on the church tower. It had been twenty-past eleven when he first looked out of this window years ago, and it was still twenty-past eleven.

There was a knock on the door. Nancy came in, smiling as usual from ear to ear. 'Jimmy won't be back for another ten days,' she said. 'So there's only five of us here – me, you, Gerald, Samantha and Teresa – ooh, and Leo of course,' she giggled. Then came the laugh and the cough. 'Excuse *me*,' she said. Leo was her unpleasantly fat dachshund that was always the wrong side of every door, that yapped hysterically every time the telephone rang and went berserk whenever the lavatory chain was pulled. Nancy loved it though, and it was never wise to call it a low-slung sausage-dog with a nasty temper, however strongly you felt about it – and George did feel very strongly about it.

The dining-room seemed even bigger after the kitchen at the Dyers'. Usually there were over twenty of them around the heavy polished table, but now the five of them were grouped down one end and Samantha couldn't manage her spaghetti. She could never manage anything. George finished and watched the others struggling on, Nancy clucking round them, cutting up and feeding and still laughing. George wondered why she did it. Teresa bit her tongue and began crying, her mouth opening under her screwed-up eyes. George had to look away while Nancy blew her nose for her and calmed her down so that Teresa could swallow what was already in her mouth.

It was an entire world away from the farm and the Dyers. George had been numbed by the speed of his return, and it was only now that he began to think of Tom and Storme. He slid along the bench, took his plate and his mug to the hatch and slipped out, the heavy front door banging behind him, harder than he had intended. The rain had stopped and the mosquitoes were out celebrating in ever-moving bunches that seemed to follow him all the way across the gravel path, past the rhododendrons to the mossy wall behind. He reached for the top and hauled himself up, scraping his shoes on the bricks. Nancy was always at him about scuffing his shoes and climbing the wall. 'We've had too many complaints, George, too many. People don't like being stared at, you know.' But the wall was his place. For hours on end he'd sit on the cold, damp bricks, swinging his legs and drumming his heels on the other side. The best time was as it was now – a summer evening with the village street to himself and only the wood pigeons above him for company. Safely in the distance he could hear shouting and laughing on the recreation ground. He settled on his wall and struck up a rhythm with his heels.

To have something to look forward to was disturbing, he decided. When he'd come back before, from other homes and holidays, there had been his room, his own books and his wall, and that was enough; the only longing he had experienced was to get back inside the familiar confines of the Home. Now everything had changed. Images flashed through his mind – Jemima sucking at Tom's shirt, the oily blackness of the floodwater in the meadow, holding on to Jemima's tail, sweating under the corrugated roof of the Dutch barn, tea round the kitchen table, the warmth of Mrs Dyer's smile, Storme hobbling round the stone circle in the mist, Tom winking at him as he was driven away that afternoon.

The mosquitoes had found him again. He stood up on the wall, arms flailing at them and walked, arms outstretched like a tightrope-walker, towards the gateway. A quick double-back-somersault on the bar, he thought, and he kicked out his feet pointing his toes like a gymnast. From the other side of the street he heard clapping. He looked up. It was the people who ran the village shop, they were leaning out of their window clapping and laughing. He was a bit taken aback at first and wondered how long they'd been spying on him. He laughed with them and tried a curtsey. He lost his balance, wobbled briefly and fell backwards off the wall. He scrambled to his feet, brushed off the leaves and ran back through the jungle of rhododendrons to the path by the front door.

Once back in the privacy of his room, he tore out a centre page of an old school exercise book, spread it out on his table and began to draw an eight-day calendar – Sunday to Sunday. Tuesday he marked with a red asterisk and wrote 'Tom sees his Mum,' and on Thursday he wrote in 'Letter from Tom'.

There were steps outside his door and then a knock. 'Are you in there, George?'

He pushed the calendar into the waste-paper basket under the table and coughed to cover the rustle of paper.

'Can I come in?' Nancy asked. She was always very particular about knocking. She and George had had a row about it some years before. She peered tentatively round the door. 'Hullo, George,' she said, looking him over seriously. 'Are you all right?'

' 'Course. Why shouldn't I be?' George said.

'It's the Beaumonts from across the road, you know, the shop people. He said you were playing up on that wall again and you fell off. He was ringing up to find out if you were all right.'

'I'm fine,' George smiled at her. 'I was just practising – gymnastics.'

'So they said.' She sounded reproving, and George prepared himself for a ticking-off.

'You shouldn't, George,' she said. 'I mean, what would happen if you fell the other side? It's straight on to the road, you know. And the little ones – if they see you, they'll only copy you. Please, George.'

'Sorry, Nan.' She liked being called Nan.

'You can always go out, I've told you, haven't I – as long as you're in before a quarter-past nine, before it's dark. I told you that at the beginning of the holidays, didn't I?'

'Yes, Nan.'

'Don't you want to go out?' Nancy said. 'Most young lads of your age can't wait to get out and about.'

'I'm going to, Nan,' George said, looking her straight in the eye. 'You'll see, Nan. I'm going to.'

Nancy didn't know what else to say. She backed out, the door closed and George heard her coughing her way downstairs again. He retrieved his crumpled calendar from the waste-paper basket, smoothed it out on the table and began to cross out the first Sunday.

Nancy was frightened of George. He was older than any other child in the Home and unlike anyone else she'd ever come across. She had been housemother at Stelling House for four years now, and in all that time she never felt confident with him. She'd tried to get through to him, to understand him, but there had never been any response. He seemed to live a separate life, removed and distant from everyone around him. Yet he was never unkind or aloof; he simply existed quite happily on his own. Time and again he'd come back from foster homes that hadn't worked out for him, and each time he just slotted back easily into the routine of the Home as if he'd never been away, as if nothing had happened.

Only once had she caught a glimpse of what was under the surface. Not long after she first came she walked into his room without knocking and found George curled up on his bed. She thought he had been crying, but there was no chance to find out. He leapt off the bed, screaming at her that this was his room and that she couldn't just wander in when she felt like it. She had caught him with his guard down.

There had been long conferences about him with Mrs Thomas, arranging holidays and foster parents. But nothing seemed to change him, he remained polite, but utterly remote and inside himself.

The calendar didn't help. George checked it several times each day, and promised himself he wouldn't cross out the day until after supper each evening. By Wednesday afternoon he had already crossed off Thursday in advance – it looked better that way.

He spent most of the time in his room trying to read, but his eyes wouldn't stay on the page. Downstairs, television was no better and there was the added distraction of the three children playing hospitals between him and the television. Nothing seemed to be able to stop the same recurring hope from interrupting his concentration. This time next week he could be back with Tom and Storme, and this time for good – not just a visit, not as an outsider but as one of the family. But the more he thought about it the more his hopes faded. He remembered Tom's reassurances and promises, and he believed in Tom, or was he forcing himself to believe what he wanted to believe? At least the letter would be here soon. Tom had said he would write, and then he would know, one way or the other. But none of this helped him to sleep that night.

Morning did come in the end, and George was downstairs early, waiting in the kitchen for Leo to go mad at the first sound of the postman's bike on the path outside. Nancy was boiling some eggs and sipping a cup of tea.

'You're down early, George,' she said. 'Cup of tea?'

George nodded, peering through the glass panes on the door.

'Leo's out there,' Nancy was beginning her laugh. 'He has a problem when it's raining – he can't make up his mind which is more important, getting the postman's ankle or keeping out of the rain. So what does he do, the poppet? He hides under my car in the dry and ambushes poor Mr Stacey as he comes past.' She squealed with laughter and had to put the teapot down as the laugh faltered, spluttered and turned into a cough. 'Oh dear, excuse *me*,' she said.

'It hasn't come yet, has it?'

'What, dear?'

'The post, Nan.'

'You'd have heard if it had, believe you me.' She handed George a cup of tea. 'Here you are now, dear. Drink it while it's hot.'

George stared through the door and sipped his tea. Nancy asked him to watch the toast while she went to help the little ones get up. He was just on the point of going to turn the toast over when he heard Leo. The postman had arrived.

George pulled open the door and Leo came scuttling in, yapping terrible threats at the postman from behind George's legs.

'Lovely little fellow, isn't he?' the postman said and handed George a small bundle of letters tied with an elastic band.

'It's not mine,' said George, disowning Leo hastily.

The postman cast his eyes to heaven and shuffled off back towards his bike. George closed the door and tugged at the elastic band. The bundle came apart untidily on the table and George pushed them aside one by one searching for his name, while Leo waddled away to his basket still grunting with satisfaction at seeing the postman off yet again.

George looked through the letters three times to be sure, but he was right the first time – they were all for Nancy, there was nothing for him. Nancy was back in the kitchen and waving frantically at a cloud of blue smoke that rose from the stove. 'Oh, George. I asked you, I asked you to watch the toast. Look at it. It's such a waste.' She looked at George and saw he wasn't listening. He was leaning on the kitchen table, and staring disconsolately down at some letters. 'Were you expecting one, George?' she asked, regretting she hadn't noticed him before the toast. George said nothing, but collected the letters together and handed them to Nancy as he brushed past her on his way upstairs.

His bed squeaked as he sat down. Tom had said he'd write on Tuesday after he'd been to the hospital, he said it would get to George by Thursday morning at the latest. But there was no letter. If Tom had written a letter, it would have to be here by now. Perhaps he hadn't written at all, perhaps he never intended to. George's worst doubts were being confirmed. Could it be that Tom had not meant what he said? Could it be that they were just trying to be kind, that they didn't really want him back at all? Could it all have been an elaborate hoax to make him feel better about being sent away? And what about Storme, could she have taken part in the deception? Tom could have done it without telling her, couldn't he? But he wasn't like that – he'd never been anything but straight; he said what he thought about having a succession of foster children to stay – why should he be pretending now? And what about the arguments with his father? They were real enough, weren't they? They couldn't have been pretending to have a row just so that he could hear them.

Someone was banging on his door. 'Nancy says it's breakfast and it's cold already.' It was Gerald's thin, whiney voice.

'Coming,' said George. There was always the second post that afternoon. Perhaps Tom put a second-class stamp on it, or perhaps he just missed the post.

'Are you coming?' Gerald was still outside his door. 'Nancy says the egg will be hard . . .' George jerked open the door and Gerald fled downstairs, shouting for Nancy.

But the postman did not even come that afternoon, nor the next morning.

To Nancy he seemed more solitary than she had ever known him. Once or twice he'd even snapped at Gerald and Teresa when they pestered him to play with them – something she'd never seen him do before. He disappeared for most of the day, but when he was with them at meals or in the playroom he seemed pre-occupied and on edge. Nancy diagnosed boredom, and set about finding tasks for George around the garden, anything that will keep him occupied, she thought. But the only one he persevered with was the mowing – the rest he gave up almost before he started. It was while he was mowing the long grass in the apple orchard behind the house that Mrs Thomas arrived.

Nancy was shouting something at him and waving her arms. George pushed down the throttle and brought the mower to a standstill. He still couldn't hear her, so he throttled down completely and the motor chugged away to nothing and there was silence all around him. Everything seemed quiet and still.

'George!' Nancy was calling him. 'It's Mrs Thomas – she's come to take you out.' George turned the machine to push it back to the shed

'Don't you bother with that,' Nancy said. 'I'll do it.'

He found Mrs Thomas by her car round the front of the house. There was nothing unusual about a visit from Mrs Thomas. She was always dropping in from time to time, sometimes just for a chat and sometimes to take him out somewhere for a drive. Normally her visits were a welcome break for him, something different, but not today. Mrs Thomas reminded him of the farm and the Dyers, and since breakfast he had managed to become completely involved in his mowing, concentrating on keeping the lines straight, on shaving the grass as close to the trees as possible. The summer smell of new mown grass was on his hands and the noise of the mower helped to obliterate all thoughts of Tom's letter. Now Mrs Thomas had brought it all back to him.

George had never felt less like talking, and since Mrs Thomas seemed quite happy talking away to herself, he was quite content to let her continue. 'Well, George,' she said after a bit. 'And what have you been doing with yourself?'

'Nothing much.' It was the truth, but George knew it sounded abrupt. It was too abrupt for Mrs Thomas who was left with nothing to say for a moment.

'I saw a friend of yours yesterday,' she said. George looked across at her.

'What friend?'

'Mrs Dyer. I went to see how she was. Poor dear – she's flat on her back still, but she's the picture of health otherwise – rosy cheeks, bright eyes. Doctor says she could be home by tomorrow. They need the beds or something, and it's not nearly as bad as they thought at first.'

'Did she say anything about me?' George tried not to sound too anxious.

'She's taken quite a shine to you, I think. You really must have behaved yourself for a change.' She smiled at him.

'That all?'

'She couldn't stop talking about you and Storme and how well you looked after her that night on the moor.'

'Nothing else?'

'What more do you want?' Mrs Thomas laughed.

'Anything about Tom or Storme?'

'Nothing special, I don't think. She hasn't seen them since last weekend. They're staying at . . .'

'When did you go? To the hospital, I mean.'

'I told you, George, yesterday – Thursday.'

'And he hadn't been in to visit her?'

'Who?'

'Tom,' said George. 'Has Tom been to see her?' He was no longer trying to be calm.

'Neither of them as far as I know. I told you.' Mrs Thomas glanced across at him, trying to understand the urgency in his questions, but George had turned his face away.

'Is everything all right, George?' she asked, but George said nothing. 'Is it about the Dyers, George?' she went on gently. 'I know you didn't want to leave, and I can tell you they certainly didn't want you to go. It was such a pity, but I know they'll want to have you back – Mrs Dyer said as much only yesterday.'

George never mentioned the Dyers or the farm again, but he thought about little else. By the time Mrs Thomas left him at the door of the Home, he knew exactly what he was going to do.

There was an old map in among the books in the playroom. George remembered that much, but it took him an age to find it. He opened it out on his bed and looked for Spreyton, the village nearest the Dyers' farm – he could find his way to their house from there. There was only one way to find out what was going on. He'd go and see them, put it to them face to face. Then, at least, he would know for sure.

He woke at first light the next morning, dressed silently and tiptoed his way down the creaky stairs to the front door – the back door was guarded by Leo. He closed the heavy door after him, wincing as he released the handle and the latch clicked into place.

Outside, a mist hung over the village. He walked quietly along the road towards the open countryside, past the still-sleeping houses. It was going to be a hot day.

CHAPTER 10

TO START WITH, GEORGE KEPT TO THE MAIN road. There were more cars and he felt he was more likely to hitch a lift than if he took the more direct route down the country roads. But nothing seemed to want to stop for him, except one tractor that trundled along for half a mile and then dropped him off again. In the first hour or so there was very little on the roads anyway, but even after that with traffic flowing past him almost continuously, no one paid any attention to him. By nine o'clock his feet were hurting, his hitching arm ached and he'd not yet reached the next little black dot on the map. His stomach rumbled and he began to wish he'd never left the Home.

He promised himself a rest after he passed the next village – unless he picked up a lift before that. But to hitch successfully you have to be an optimist, and George had lost his optimism miles back. Now he no longer bothered to turn his head and look round when he heard an engine behind him. His shoulder moved automatically, following his hooked thumb in slow, tired circles. It was this that brought about the only light relief of the morning, when the hum of an engine behind him turned out to be a long black shiny hearse containing two bald undertakers in the front, and presumably someone else in the flower-covered coffin in the back. George was still chuckling to himself when a white car with 'Police' written on it pulled up beside him.

George wasn't frightened of policemen. He just thought they were strange – straight out of *The Bill*, not like real people somehow; and when they had their hats off like the one who was speaking to him now, they were even more unreal. He wondered if they were after him for hitching the hearse.

'Where you off to, son? Exeter?' He was a sergeant, three stripes on his arm. They were both looking at him. George nodded. It was all he could think to do.

'What's your name then?' The police radio crackled out a curt message.

'Tom,' he said, lying easily.

'Tom what?'

'Tom Dyer.' It was only after he'd lied that he realised why he'd done so. Quite suddenly it occurred to him that the policemen were a threat – that Nancy might have rung them up, told them he'd run off. He stepped back from the car, hoping it would drive off, that there would be no more questions; but instead, the back door opened and he found himself sitting in the police car on his way to Exeter, which was miles out of his way.

'Where you from, son?' the sergeant said, swivelling round to face him. George almost looked down at his map which was still open on his knees, but he stopped himself just in time.

'Crediton,' he said – he'd passed the sign a couple of miles back.

'You haven't walked far then?' said the driver, not turning his head.

'No.'

'You live there?' The driver wasn't asking out of interest. George knew he was being questioned.

'No,' he said. 'My aunt lives there. I've been staying with her.' The story seemed to come easily.

'Where's your home then?' The sergeant this time.

'Spreyton.'

'What you off to Exeter for then?' The driver again.

'To see my mother – she's in hospital.' The sergeant was still scrutinising him – he could feel it. 'She's hurt her back.'

'Sorry to hear that, son.' The tone was less aggressive now. 'Which hospital is it?' George was searching his memory frantically – he'd only been there last Saturday – but nothing came. The police radio saved him from his confusion, breaking into the purr of the car and turning the sergeant's face away from him at last.

'Four one. Go ahead.'

It was a welcome break for George, a chance to collect his thoughts and recover his composure. The sergeant was still talking on the radio. George glanced down at his map. They'd be in Exeter soon. He tried to follow the road from Exeter to Spreyton, but the movement of the car made it difficult and he began to feel sick. He'd never been able to read in a car, the slightest effort to concentrate on a page turned his stomach. He looked away, swallowing back the saliva that had come up into his mouth and praying he wouldn't be sick. The sergeant was looking at him.

'You all right, son?' he said. 'You look as if you've seen a ghost.'

'I'm fine.' George hardly dared to open his mouth.

'She must be in the Wonford Hospital,' the driver said. George tried to see what his face looked like in the driving mirror, but the mirror was at the wrong angle for him.

'Is that the place, son?' The sergeant was studying his face. The nausea was passing off now, and George was trying to take in what he was saying.

'What?'

'Your mum. Jeff here thinks it'll be the Wonford she's in. Is that right?'

George still couldn't remember, but he nodded just the same.

'My brother was in there, with his neck,' the driver said. 'We go right past it on the way to the station.'

They left him alone after that and George looked out of the car window watching the countryside turning to regular rows of red-brick houses. They passed the 'Welcome to Exeter' sign and a few minutes later turned through the gates into the forecourt of the hospital. George recognised it immediately – it was the same hospital. Mrs Dyer was in there and she would tell him everything he wanted to know. She liked him. Tom said so, Mrs Thomas said so.

'Here you are then, son, delivered to the door,' the sergeant said, smiling at him. 'Hope your mum's better.'

'Thanks,' said George. The driver turned round for the first time. He was looking hard at George.

'Off you go then,' he said. 'You don't want to keep her waiting, do you?'

George saw a flicker of suspicion in his hard grey eyes, and heard it in his voice. George looked away, fumbled with the door lock, tried the window lever and finally pulled out the ashtray. The sergeant stretched across him and opened the door. 'Thanks for the lift,' said George, relieved to be out of the car and away from the driver's eyes, and he watched the police car turn out of sight behind the hospital wall. George walked towards the entrance.

The nurse behind the desk didn't seem very interested in him. 'Miss,' he ventured, trying to attract her attention. But the nurse went on chatting to a man in a white coat. 'Excuse me,' George leaned forward. She looked at him coldly.

'Yes?'

'I want to see Mrs Dyer.'

'Private wing?'

'What?'

'Is she in the private wing?'

'I don't know – she was in a ward . . .'

She smiled secretly at the man next to her. George was beginning to feel foolish.

'Visiting hours on the wards are in the afternoons.'

'I know that, but I must . . .'

'Are you a relation?' She was tired of the conversation.

'I'm her son,' George said, listening in amazement to his own bravado. The nurse was looking down a list, following a pointed finger nail.

'Ward Seven, East Wing. Ask the staff nurse on duty – she may let you in, but I doubt it.'

George was about to ask how to get there but thought the better of it. The nurse was already chatting again to the man in the white coat. It was as if George wasn't there at all.

The way was well signposted. He found the doors to

the ward and looked around for the nurse. There was no one about. He stood up on tip-toe and peered through the glass pane at the top of the door. It was the same ward, just as he remembered it. He was searching the left-hand side of the ward – Mrs Dyer's bed had been some way down. Someone was behind him – he could sense it.

'May I help you?' George felt as if he'd been caught shoplifting.

'I'm looking for Mrs Dyer,' George said; it sounded a bit lame even to him. The ward sister was wearing a broad belt with a silver buckle and was as stiff as her uniform.

'Are you indeed?' She stepped closer to him, looking him up and down. 'And are you aware that visiting hours are in the afternoons from two to four? I make it . . .' she looked down at the watch that was dangling from her uniform, 'twenty-three minutes past eleven.'

'I only wanted . . .'

'Did you say Mrs Dyer?' Her voice lost its authoritative bite, and she spoke more quietly, more as if she expected an answer. George felt encouraged.

'Yes,' said George. 'She's in this ward, isn't she?'

'Are you a relative?'

'She's my mother. I just came in . . .'

'You're Tom then?' He nodded, but her eyes never left his face, and George had the feeling she knew something he didn't. 'Did you come from home this morning?'

'On the bus,' said George. He didn't dare look at her, but he knew he was still being scrutinised. He had to convince her. 'Dad couldn't come, see, so he sent me instead.'

'In the morning? But he knows visiting hours are in the afternoon – he's been here himself, he knows that.' George was beginning to feel trapped.

'Well, he must've forgotten,' he said. 'He told me I could visit anytime.'

'It's all very strange, very strange indeed,' she said. She was playing with him now. There was undisguised triumph in her voice. He glanced at her mouth. She was smiling, but it was not a friendly smile, it was the smile of a cat that knows it has a kill. 'You see, Tom or whatever your name is, your mother was driven home yesterday evening in an ambulance. So if she's anywhere, she's at home – and that's where you've just come from this morning, isn't it?' Somehow George was prepared for the shock. Almost before she'd finished speaking he realised that there was only one way out now – to run.

He rushed past her outstretched hand and took off down the squeaky corridor. She was shouting after him. 'Stop! Wait! Come back!' But George had turned the corner, dodging a stretcher coming the other way. No one made a move to stop him. He was aware of mouths opening and people stopping to stare as he tore past. An old lady in a wheel-chair was negotiating the exit, so he went out of the entrance, slipped between two parked ambulances and made for the main gate.

By early afternoon, with the sun beating down from a clear blue sky, his mouth dry with thirst and a caving sensation in his stomach, George reached the open countryside at last. His map had been of little use to him in Exeter, and he'd trudged round the city for hours trying to find a road out of the city to Spreyton – a village no one seemed to have heard of. One lady in a corner sweet shop told him to ask a policeman, and pointed the way to the nearest police station. George thanked her and went the other way – he'd had his fill of policemen for one day. But it was a post-man who helped him in the end – he had an uncle living in South Tawton, the next village to Spreyton. George managed to hitch a ride on the back of a builder's truck with the wind blowing cement powder all over him, and they dropped him only a mile or so from Spreyton – according to his map. It was like the end of a race. There was new strength in his legs, and he promised himself a long drink in the river by the water-meadows.

He began to recognise every bend in the road. He forgot the fur on his tongue, his blistering feet and his throbbing head – he was nearly there. The road straightened out in front of him and he could see the cattle grid at the top of the drive. He climbed the wall into the field and looked down into the valley towards the house. The calves were back in the water-meadows and someone was burning a bonfire behind the house. George balanced his way across the cattle grid, and ran, bent double, down the field towards the river – keeping out of sight of the house and barns.

Under the cover of the bank behind him, George knelt on all fours like an animal and plunged his face into the river. He drank until he could drink no more, but his face still needed the cool of the water, so he pushed his whole head under and held his breath as long as he could. He held it too long and came up spluttering and coughing, but as the water stilled and his breathing came more easily, his eyes focused on a reflection in the water. A voice behind him confirmed that his eyes were not playing tricks on him. It was Tom's voice.

'You've taken your time, haven't you?'

'Tom! How did . . .'

'Saw you up by the cattle grid, watched you coming across the field like a commando, and here you are. Mind you, we expected you for lunch – what kept you?'

'You knew I was coming?' George stood up and felt the drips running off his nose.

'The phone hasn't stopped all day – first of all Mrs Thomas, then the police, then the hospital. We've had a sort of running commentary. I told Mum you'd be here by lunch-time. She was getting quite worried, thought you'd got yourself lost or run over or something.' Tom laughed. 'You should see yourself, George. And what have you been eating, cement?

Mum'll have a fit when she sees those clothes – could put her back out again.'

George was still trying to get used to him again, trying to gauge the tone in his voice. Was it forced jollity to cover up his embarrassment? Was he really pleased to see him? Almost not wanting to hear the answer, he blurted out the question that had plagued him all week.

'Tom, what happened?'

'What do you mean?'

'The letter. I never got the letter you promised and you never went to see your mother like you said you would.'

'Oh, that. Yes, I'm sorry about all that, George, but we had a change of plan, and I wasn't allowed to tell you.'

'Change of plan?'

'Not a plan really. Things just happened differently, that's all.'

'What do you mean?'

'Well I told Dad, the day after you left. It was by accident really – we were fixing up the pens for the dipping.'

'Dipping?'

'Sheep-dipping. Anyway, it just slipped out. We were talking about you and Dad was sort of apologising for what had happened and then out it came. I told him that Storme and me were serious and we wanted you to come and live here full time. It was strange really, because he didn't seem a bit surprised, said that if that's what we felt he'd go into Exeter the next day and talk to Mum. And he did.'

'What did she say?' George couldn't contain himself any longer. 'Tell me what she said.'

'She just said we had to think about it – all of us.'

'Think about it?'

'Mum was coming out of hospital Friday evening – yesterday that was – we could all think about it and in the meantime Mum said she'd have a word with your Mrs Thomas.'

'But Mrs Thomas, she never said anything to me about . . .'

'She wasn't allowed to. No one was allowed to. Dad made everyone promise not to tell you anything till it was all decided for sure. That's why I didn't write, see?'

'What did you decide?' George asked, knowing the answer now, but longing to hear the sound of it.

Tom smiled at him and George knew that there was no doubt any more. 'What do you think?' he said. 'I can't tell you. We agreed Storme should be the one to tell you. I warn you, she'll cry. She always cries when she's happy. Come on, they're all waiting up there, biting their nails and drinking pots of tea.'

Jemima was back in the water-meadows and followed them all the way across the field to the track that led up towards the farmhouse. As they climbed the gate George was telling him about the ward sister at the hospital. He jumped down and waited for Tom. There was a shriek of joy from the direction of the house. Storme was coming for him, leaping from rut to rut, her hair sweeping the air behind her.

'Here it comes,' said Tom. 'Your own live sister – do you really know what you've taken on?'

'Haven't got any choice, have I?'

'Not really,' said Tom. 'I never had any choice either – take it or leave it.'

'I'll take it,' said George, watching Storme springing like a deer from side to side. 'Her ankle looks better.'

'Everything's better,' said Tom.

Which type of book do you like best?

Take the quiz . . . then read the book!

Who would you like to have an adventure with?
a) On my own
b) A ghost
c) Someone in my family
d) My best friend
e) My pet

Where would you like to go on holiday?
a) A remote island or a far-away mountain
b) A fantasy world
c) Anywhere as long as my family and friends are there
d) A different time period
e) The countryside

I would like to be an . . .
a) Explorer
b) Author
c) Someone who helps others
d) Warrior
e) Circus ringmaster

My favourite stories are . . .
a) Full of adventure
b) Magical
c) About friendships and family
d) War stories
e) About animals

If you answered mostly with A you'll enjoy . . .

KENSUKE'S KINGDOM

Washed up on an island
with no food and water,
Michael cannot survive.
But he is not alone . . .

If you answered mostly with B you'll enjoy . . .

THE GHOST OF GRANIA O'MALLEY

There is gold in the Big
Hill, but Jessie and Jake
can't bear for the hill to be
destroyed. Can they save it
before it's too late?

If you answered mostly with C you'll enjoy . . .

MR NOBODY'S EYES

Harry befriends Ocky, a chimpanzee from the circus. Harry and the chimp are on the run, but now things aren't turning out as Harry planned!

If you answered mostly with D you'll enjoy . . .

FRIEND OR FOE

It is the Blitz. One night David and his friend see a German plane crash on the moors. Do they leave the airmen to die?

If you answered mostly with E you'll enjoy . . .

WAR HORSE

In the deadly chaos of the
First World War, one horse
witnesses the reality of
battle from both sides of
the trenches.

MICHAEL MORPURGO
The master storyteller